HIS BABYGIRL

Boston Doms - Book Four

JANE HENRY
MAISY ARCHER

Published by Blushing Books
An Imprint of
ABCD Graphics and Design, Inc.
A Virginia Corporation
977 Seminole Trail #233
Charlottesville, VA 22901

Jane Henry and Maisy Archer
His Babygirl

EBook ISBN: 978-1-68259-923-5
Print ISBN: 978-1-64563-162-0
v1

Chapter 1

Alice darted a nervous glance up and down the quiet street. After assuring herself that it was completely deserted, she put a slightly crumpled cigarette between her lips and lit it. As she inhaled deeply, letting the acrid smoke sear a path down her throat and into her lungs, she felt something inside her loosen and rolled her eyes at her own behavior.

Sneaking around like you're sixteen again, Alice?

She reminded herself that smoking, while hardly the healthiest choice for many reasons, was not *illegal* for God's sake—not even in Boston, so long as she stayed away from building entrances. And if the residents here on Queensborough Street—a mixture of professionals from the nearby medical center and students from the multitude of surrounding colleges—wanted to clutch their collective pearls about anything that happened on the street this evening, they had bigger things to gripe about than a lone woman leaning against a lamppost and having a cigarette break.

She wondered how many of the residents knew that the unassuming, unmarked brownstone with the small, shabby bar beneath it was actually the home of The Club, the BDSM play-

ground so well-known and respected in the Boston D/s community that it didn't need any other name. If the neighbors knew,
they kept the information to themselves.

It helped that Master Blake, The Club's current owner, had
invested God-only-knew how much money in getting the place
secured and soundproofed. She knew for a fact that inside the
building was a cacophony of music and laughter. Out here,
though, even just a few feet from the entrance, all she could hear
was the noise of cars passing in the distance and the whistle of
the bitingly cold wind as it whipped between the buildings,
making the little white Christmas lights on the trees dance and
sway. And with all of his high-tech cameras monitoring the place
from every angle, Blake had made Queensborough one of the
safest streets in Boston.

A scuffle of sound to her right made her whirl on the spot,
her heart pounding, but when she turned… nothing.

Gah! What a ninny! She would *not* jump like an idiot every time
a dead leaf blew across the sidewalk. She was a mature, adult
woman who made her own decisions, for better or worse. She
answered to no one but herself.

She ground her teeth together and deliberately took another
deep drag.

She knew exactly who she was afraid would catch her smoking, and the knowledge made her want to shake herself. It
wasn't the neighbors she worried about disappointing, nor her
boss, nor one of her friends. It wasn't her parents, even though
they'd probably rant about how this was another sign of her
moral weakness, the way they had about almost every decision
she'd made since the fateful night almost seven years ago when
she'd lost her virginity and gotten pregnant all in one fell
swoop. It wasn't even her own six-year-old son, Charlie, who
knew enough about the dangers of smoking that she'd have to
do some pretty quick verbal tap dancing to explain herself. No,
she was worried that she'd disappoint the one person whose

opinion she should care about the *least*—Alexander "Slay" Slater.

Why should she worry about disappointing someone who had made it overwhelmingly clear that he didn't want her to be accountable to him?

She wondered sometimes whether Slay's attitude towards her was her own fault. Since she'd started working at The Club as a bartender last spring, she'd had the most overwhelming crush on him. And God, who could blame her? He was six feet, five inches of hard, tattooed muscle, and everything from his shaved head to his piercings to his heavy motorcycle boots screamed *badass*. He was a restless, broody tattoo artist with eyes that said he'd seen and done terrible things and needed comfort she instinctively wanted to provide. He was a former Marine and Dungeon Master with an inherent need to lead and command. The sexual submissive inside her couldn't help but respond. And if all of that weren't enough? He was some kind of undercover-operations-hero who'd helped rescue not one but *two* of her friends from sketchy, dangerous situations in the last year, and gotten himself shot (yes, *shot*!) in the arm in the process. For a girl who'd grown up in a household so conservative it made 1950s sitcoms look edgy, he was the ultimate bad boy fantasy.

So, she'd followed him around like an obedient little puppy, hanging on his every command, unable to stop herself from trying to please him. *You want me to work the stupid outer bar at The Club where nobody tips and nothing fun ever happens? Yes, sir, Slay, whatever you say! You want me to stay out of the playrooms during my off-time, and never participate in any of the scenes? Sure thing, no problem!*

And what had that cooperative, submissive attitude gotten her? A thinner wallet than any other bartender or waitress at The Club, and a case of sexual frustration so bad that she couldn't stand it. Meanwhile, *Slay* had gone off and made a play for Hillary, the girl his best friend Matteo Angelico had been trying *not* to fall for. And when that didn't work out for Slay, and

Matt and Hillie finally got together (because *duh*, anyone with eyes could see that Hillie and Matt were meant to be, no matter how hard Matt had tried to fight it), Slay had gone on a man-whoring rampage, doing scenes with every skank who expressed the slightest interest in him and making sure that Alice knew *all* about them. And just in case she hadn't gotten the message that he had no interest in her whatsoever, he'd taken it one step further and had gone out of his way to avoid conversation with her since October.

Since he'd been shot.

Since she'd rushed to the hospital to sit by his bedside and had been firmly rejected.

So, screw him. The crush was officially *over*, and so was her desire to obey him.

Since Slay was Master Blake's right-hand man, Alice still had to be professional and polite, of course. But over the last month or two, she'd deliberately stopped following his every order as if it were gospel. Now she worked the *real* bar, in the members-only part of the club (for which her wallet cheered), and she definitely participated in the scenes from time to time. Nothing serious, nothing hardcore—a good spanking, a little rope play, but enough to take the edge off.

And if she noticed that Slay's jaw got hard and his eyes smoldered a bit when he heard about her participating in a scene, she ruthlessly squashed the instinctive desire to back down. Honestly, there were a multitude of things in this life that she was powerless to control—her ultra-religious family, the rich bitches who ran Pevrell and Brahms where Charlie went to school, the way her landlord was always around when it was time to raise the rent but never when she needed things repaired—and it was nice to feel like she still had *some* power over her own life.

Even if the only thing she could control was having a damn cigarette when she felt like it.

She took another deep drag and held it until her lungs were

ready to burst, then slowly exhaled. It was like a Zen meditation thing, only much less healthy.

"Was it good?"

The deep, soft voice made her drop the cigarette and spin on the spot, sinking into the fighting stance she'd learned in her high school self-defense class.

Slay ran his gaze over her pose and snorted dismissively. His arms were folded across his chest in a casual way, but there was nothing relaxed about the tension in his shoulders or the tight set of his jaw.

"Damn it, Slay!" Alice said angrily. She stood up straight again, and laid a hand over her chest, where her heart was still pounding crazily. A man as big as Slay should move like a lumbering elephant, not a fucking ghost.

Slay took a step forward, placing himself between her and The Club. He deliberately put his boot over the butt of her cigarette, which still smoldered on the sidewalk, and twisted his foot.

Alice shut her eyes and sighed. Of course it was too much to hope that he'd missed the part where the cigarette was in her hand. *Cue the lecture.*

But no lecture was forthcoming. Slay just stood there, silently watching her. Assessing her. Judging her. Making her want to squirm.

It was freaking cold out here. She hadn't noticed it before, but now the early-December chill seemed to seep into her bones. The temperature didn't seem to faze Slay in the slightest—he was a veritable space heater, and her body leaned toward the palpable warmth of his before she forced herself back. She folded her own arms over her chest, mirroring his position, fighting the urge to speak under the weight of his silence.

Being immune to him was a lot easier when he was ignoring her.

Finally, she couldn't take it any longer.

"My break's almost over," she said as politely as she could, unclenching her arms and making to scoot around him to head back into the building. "So, if you'll excuse me?"

Something flared in his eyes. He nodded his head once, as if coming to a decision, and moved his big body quickly, gracefully, to block her.

So Alice stepped to his other side.

With that same fluid grace, he moved in front of her again, so close that his crossed arms nearly brushed her chest.

Alice looked up. "You have something to say?" she demanded. *Just get it over with and go back to ignoring me before my body spontaneously combusts from being so close to yours, damn it.*

Slay's eyebrows rose. "I was still waiting for you to answer *my* question."

Alice frowned. "What question?"

"I asked you if it was *good*," Slay reminded her. "That cigarette."

Alice expelled a breath. "It was *terrific*," she said flatly. "Best five minutes of my night."

Slay nodded thoughtfully. "I guess it would have to be." He pursed his lips and regarded her silently for another moment, making no move to get out of her way.

God, his Mr. Inscrutable routine was annoying. And fucking sexy. And *annoying*.

"Fine. I'll bite. What does *that* mean?" she asked, bracing her hands on her hips. The beam of the streetlight cut across his face, highlighting his eyes—golden brown, and fringed with long, thick black lashes that any supermodel would envy. On any other guy, those eyes would lock comically feminine. On Slay, they just emphasized his all-consuming masculinity—the hard angle of his jaw, the slash of his cheekbones. At the moment, she found all of *that* annoying, too.

Slay gave an exaggerated shrug as though the answer were obvious. "It means, you violated the terms of your employment.

I would imagine it would've had to be a damn good cigarette to be worthwhile."

Alice felt her jaw drop. What the hell was he talking about?

"Violated the terms of my employment?" she scoffed. "For smoking? Half the people who work here smoke." She hated that her voice sounded so high and defensive, and forced herself to stand taller.

"Mmm," he agreed. "But those people didn't put *non-smoker* on their applications." He leaned toward her just slightly, and her poor heart started hammering again, reminding her that he was nearly a foot taller than she was, and least a hundred pounds heavier; that he was a predator, and she was prey. "And to be honest, little Alice, I don't give a shit whether any of *them* smoke."

It was so tempting to twist his words, to take them to mean that she was special to him in some way. But Slay had made it clear back in his hospital room that this would never be more than a fantasy. His big brown eyes, groggy with sleep and pain meds, had opened, focused on her for one moment, and immediately filled with alarm and anger. "Jesus, Alice! Go home, you hear me?" he'd slurred. "I don't *want* you here!" A man couldn't be much clearer than that.

But Slay was the ultimate dominant. No matter how lukewarm his feelings were for her personally, his desire to protect was woven into every cell of his body, and he couldn't just turn that shit off. This little intervention was him protecting her from what he thought was a bad decision, whether she wanted his interference or not. Like she was his kid. Or his sister.

Humiliation complete. She definitely liked it better when he was just ignoring her.

"Slay," she said, pleased to hear that her voice sounded reasonable though she spoke through gritted teeth. "I appreciate that you wanna protect me, but this is not the tack to take. I know it's not healthy, but single moms only get so many vices, okay? A cigarette here and there is not a big deal. And we both know it's total bullshit to think that you could get me fired for having a cigarette. You're insulting my intelligence here, big guy."

He stared at her intently, and a slow, wide smile broke out over his face. But the smile didn't reach his molten eyes. Her heart thumped wildly.

"You sure about that, Alice? You wanna take your chances? Be my guest." He stepped to her side and swept his arm out, as though inviting her to lead them inside. Then he leaned down and whispered directly in her ear, "Let's just see what happens when I tell Blake that his employee was smoking right out in front of the building, tarnishing the image of The Club."

Alice swallowed. His hot breath on her neck was messing with her mind, making her nipples bead against the lace of her bra, making her forget her own name. It was true that most employees smoked out in the back alley, but she'd assumed that was more preference than official policy. She licked her lips nervously.

"You think people who come here to be whipped a-a-and *blindfolded* are gonna judge me for having a cigarette?" She tried to sound indignant, but her voice had gone weak and breathless just from having him close. God, he smelled amazing—like musk and wood smoke. And now she was thinking about *blindfolds*, a kink that had always been a hard limit for her, but which, in conjunction with thoughts of Slay, made her heart pound with something that felt strangely like arousal.

"I think the patrons of this club, like most people who really understand D/s, are all about safe and sane behavior." His voice was a low rumble that she felt in her belly. "There's nothing safe about smoking. And there's nothing *sane* about you standing out here arguing that fact with me when you should be apologizing instead."

The absurdity of his words cut through her arousal and she

spun to face him. "Apologizing? To *you*? For what? For making a choice, just because you don't happen to agree with it?"

Sexual frustration, sorrow, and anger were riding her, making her voice shrill. How dare he ignore her for weeks and then come after her this way!

His eyes narrowed, not too pleased with her backtalk.

Good.

"For being an idiot who doesn't take her health or her *job* seriously," he told her, his eyes hot and his expression serious as a heart attack.

"Jesus! I don't believe you. You know what, Slay? Fuck you!" she said loudly.

"Say again?"

The two words vibrated with warning, but she would not heed it. She'd already given too much of herself to people *like him* who didn't deserve it, apologized for too many things, *like this*, that didn't require apology.

"You heard me," she said, narrowing her eyes. And just in case the people across the street hadn't heard her the first time, she said it again, louder, jabbing her index finger into the hard wall of his chest as she enunciated each word. "FUCK. YOU."

A hot flush climbed up Slay's neck and suffused his cheeks, and his eyes simmered like bubbling caramel. But he stood frozen, every muscle locked down, while he stared at her and breathed in and out.

He was trying to control his temper, she realized. Why? So he could go back to ignoring her? How typical.

She made a dismissive noise and once again tried to step around him.

With one enormous hand, he reached out and grabbed her elbow, yanking her to his side, and then he led them both up the walkway and down the short flight of steps to the building entrance. He grabbed the heavy exterior door with his free hand

and pulled it back so violently that it hit the wall of the building with a loud *crash*.

Holy shit. She hadn't thought that was possible.

Her heart stuttered for a second before beating even faster, making her lightheaded and nauseous. She was a tiny bit scared… and just a tiny bit thrilled. *I made him do that*.

He led her past the security guys, Donnie and Jace, who monitored the door between the outer bar and the members-only rooms. The guys, who always greeted Alice with a friendly joke or wisecrack, looked quickly from Slay to her, and then back again. Alice couldn't see Slay's expression from this angle, but whatever was there wiped the smiles off their faces. Their eyes widened and they opened the double doors without comment.

The same process repeated as Slay led her through the main bar, the crowds parting before them. Gabby, who was working the bar during Alice's break, caught her eye and gave her a questioning glance. Alice shook her head once—*Nothing to see here!*—and tried to smile. Of course, it was difficult to look nonchalant when an ogre was leading you along by the elbow.

He led her to the back area, where the employee rooms and Blake's office were located, and for the first time, worry wormed its way through her mind. *Shit*. Could he really get her fired? It wasn't legal—she wasn't an idiot, and she knew that much. But Slay and Blake were tight, and Blake might do it if Slay asked. Not to mention, Blake seemed to have other things on his mind lately, and left the day-to-day running of The Club to Slay more often than not. And if they *did* fire her, she wasn't likely to sue The Club to get her job back, partly because she couldn't afford an attorney and partly because she needed to avoid association with The Club for Charlie's and her parents' sake.

Maybe she could get more hours at *Cara*, the Italian restaurant where she worked her second job. But she wasn't sure how long that job would even extend beyond the holidays.

"Slay, I…" she began. She was ready to apologize even though she wasn't sorry. God knew she had plenty of practice at that.

But Slay didn't lead her to Blake's office. In fact, he dragged her past it, heading to the new elevator that had been installed at the back of the building that led to the basement stock rooms and upstairs, to the private play rooms. He stretched out one long, callused finger and jabbed the Up button.

What the heck?

She wrenched her elbow away from him, or tried to. The man was a brick wall and his grip, while not painful, was as unbreakable as an iron shackle. But the second he felt her resistance, he spun her around, her back to the wall beside the elevator, and his big body moved in front of her, caging her in.

"Where are you taking me?" she demanded, staring up at him. She would *not* notice the heat and strength of him, the way his arms bracketed her so easily, the intense determination in his beautiful eyes. Damn it, *why* were his eyes so beautiful?

"Upstairs," he told her. "I'm going to take care of you."

She blinked. Then she blinked again. He hadn't said "take care of you" in a *tender* way. There was no implied love, no unspoken "baby" at the end of that sentence. Instead, he was imminently practical, a man with a job to do. There was a problem, and he was going to "take care" of it. If Slay had been a mobster, she'd have worried she was being sent to sleep with the fishes. If he were a doctor, he'd be doing surgery. But no, Slay was a *dominant*, so that meant he'd…

He'd…

Oh, wait a minute. Hold the fucking phone.

"No way. N-no *way*," she stuttered, just as the elevator dinged and the doors opened.

He grabbed her elbow, hauled her inside the tiny elevator,

and jabbed the button. Slay let go of her just before the doors slid shut.

They stared at one another across the dimly lit space, both breathing heavily.

He was going to spank her right now. Unless she said "no" clearly and forcefully, he would take her into a private room and spank her ass with those giant, rough hands. She could see the intent written on his face, plain as day, and it was like a fantasy come to life... except that in her fantasy, he'd be doing it because he wanted to, because he wanted *her*, not because he felt some weird protective obligation.

Did his motives really matter, though? In a way, it would be no different than participating in a scene with some nameless guy she'd never talk to again. She was wound tighter than a spring, and her body craved the release she could find at his hands.

But then what? Back to business as usual, being co-workers? Could he do that? Could *she*?

Alice was breathing hard, swallowing convulsively, and she was mortified to find that her knees were weak. Slay... well, Slay was a wall, showing all the emotion of concrete, except for his eyes, which lit with challenge.

You wanted this, Alice. So take it.

She threw her head back and met his gaze defiantly, saying nothing.

The elevator dinged again, and the doors slid open smoothly. Alice was prepared for him to take her elbow again, but he didn't. Instead, he cocked his head to the side, waiting for her to move in front of him.

Another challenge? Right. Nothing would happen now without her consent.

She stepped out into the hallway.

He did take her elbow again, then, gently leading her down the hall and pulling his master key from his pocket to unlock the door. She took a deep breath and took a step forward.

Inside, a single weak lamp glowed in the corner, illuminating the shape of the room—the bed, a small table, a spanking bench, the door that led to a small private bathroom. The room was bare but for the furniture, a blank canvas for a dom's imagination. Most of the doms who rented the rooms did so in advance and for a specific purpose, to set up a specific scene. Most brought their own props and implements, though Blake would supply larger equipment on request. It was obvious that the room hadn't been used recently… and that no one had planned to use it tonight. The air inside was chilly and stale, and Alice shivered, wishing she could feel Slay's body heat again.

Was she going to do this? Let him spank her? It was what she'd wanted for months, wasn't it? Should she tell him her hard limits? That she didn't like restraints, she wasn't into any hardcore kink like breath play, and for some reason, she'd never been able to tolerate sensory deprivation, like blindfolds?

Slay moved in behind her and the door shut behind him with a soft click. Without saying a word, he reached for the thermostat on the wall and bumped the temperature up several degrees.

He'd seen her shiver and he was keeping her safe and comfortable. But without touching her, naturally. Keeping his distance.

And that wasn't what she wanted at all.

Alice sighed, and felt her shoulders slump, at once tired and defeated. "Slay, I can't do this."

"Face the wall and spread your legs."

Alice turned to find him leaning back against the door, his arms folded over his chest, his face impassive and his eyes… burning.

She shook her head quickly. "No. This isn't what I want."

Before she had time to think, he was behind her, turning her. One strong forearm wrapped around her stomach, holding her against him, while the other braced them against the wall. He tilted her head to the side with his chin and whispered in her ear.

"Bullshit, baby. You wanted this. You wanted *exactly* this. That's why you've defied me for the past few months, working the main bar, wearing this skimpy leather skirt. And that's why you went outside tonight. You knew every inch of this building is covered by security cameras. You knew I'd see you, that I'd come for you, that I'd spank you. You know that you need this from me."

Oh, *God*. Where was the instant denial that should be coming to her lips? Where was the outrage? She couldn't summon any. Maybe she *had* known.

"Spread your legs for me, Alice," he commanded softly. "Take your punishment."

As though her muscles obeyed his command without consulting her brain, her feet moved apart, and when he placed his hand against the small of her back and pushed gently, she arched forward.

"That's my girl," he approved, and Alice felt a brief flare of pleasure at his words. Then Slay grasped her hips and pulled her ass back against him, and her thoughts completely stuttered to a halt.

Oh my God. Pressed against her was a rock-hard erection that, like everything about Slay, was of mammoth proportion. And she knew in that instant that he wasn't simply a little turned on by their positions, and he wasn't just understandably excited by the impending spanking, like any dom might be. No, he was violently, rampantly aroused in a way that said he'd been suffering this way for more than a minute or two. He was hard as stone, for *her*. This wasn't just about his instinctive need to protect her from herself, and he definitely wasn't thinking of her as a sister.

And that changed everything.

From one second to the next, she surrendered completely. And she knew he felt it when he stepped back, no longer fighting her or even commanding her, but arranging her pliant limbs into the proper position, bending her at just the right angle.

She closed her eyes and listened to his harsh breathing, concentrated on the tingles of sensation she felt when his fingers brushed against her skin. She was so turned on that her pussy throbbed with it. She needed his hands on her *right that second*.

He knelt behind her, his hands guiding her high-heeled feet just a few inches further apart, and then he stopped. His hands dragged up the insides of her bare legs, from her ankles up her smooth calves to her knees, and then further, along the backs of her thighs to the hem of her short black leather skirt, now pulled taut against her spread legs. He stood up, hooked his fingers under the hem and lifted it, centimeter by centimeter, exposing the swell of her ass, shielded only by the tiniest scrap of black lace, to his eyes.

He was going to punish her, and she was going to let him.

It was exquisite torture waiting for that first slap to land, imagining his eyes on her flesh, wondering what he thought and whether he could possibly be as turned on as she was.

And then his broad, hot palm hit her cool flesh, and she could think of nothing but that.

Holy shit, but it hurt.

Maybe it was because her emotions were running high, or maybe because she hadn't had a good session in weeks, but the pain was startling in its intensity. In the two years she'd been into the club scene, out of the dozen or more guys who had spanked her ass in that time, she'd never felt the pain come on so swiftly and powerfully.

"You messed up tonight, little girl," he told her. She gritted her teeth as he blistered her backside with a half-dozen stinging swats that echoed around the nearly empty room.

Alice frowned. What had he said? The pain made it hard to focus.

"Uh. Yes. Yes, sir. Sorry." She recited her expected line dutifully.

But from behind her, she heard Slay mutter "*Jesus*," clearly not appeased by her rote recitation. He leaned over and whispered hotly into her ear, "When I'm punishing you, you call me Daddy. Understood?"

"What?" she whispered. *Daddy?* Her brain instantly rejected the idea, even as her belly flipped and her thighs clenched.

She'd heard of daddy doms in the past, had known a couple of girls who got off on playing the babygirl, but had never found it remotely appealing... until now. Until *Slay*, who was obviously not playing around.

He spanked her lower this time, delivering a stinging slap to the area just above her thighs. "You heard me, Alice. Say *yes, Daddy.*"

"Ow!" she complained. "Calm down!" She needed a minute to remember all the reasons why she couldn't say it, *shouldn't* say it, no matter how tempting it was.

"Try. One. More. Time," he said, the sound of his hand on her ass punctuating each word. His voice was harsher now, impatient with her stalling tactics. "*Yes, Daddy.*"

Could she? Another searing swat had her nearly blubbering, but when she spoke, it wasn't the pain talking, but something deeper. A longing inside her.

"Yes, Daddy!"

She closed her eyes as his hand stilled. His voice was deeper, but softer, as he spoke. "That's right, baby," he told her. His spanking hand paused, kneading her backside, while the other wrapped around under her arm to grip her chin and turn her gaze toward his. "*Daddy*. Not some random asshole you've picked up downstairs. Not some piece of shit who's spanking your ass just because he gets off on the experience and you wanna scratch an itch. But an honest-to-God dominant who expects you to take your safety seriously. Things are changing, baby. I've bided my time, but I'm not waiting any longer. After tonight, you belong to me. Do you understand your daddy?"

She didn't understand a damn thing, but she nodded as much as she could with his hand holding her chin.

Slay sighed and released his grip. "You don't. But you will, baby. You will."

He placed one broad palm against the small of her back, keeping her arched so that her ass was thrust out, while the other one came down quick and hard on the top of her thighs.

Holy crap.

"Slay... *Daddy!*" she shouted, wrenching one hand off the wall and moving it to shield herself. "You're doing it wrong! That's too hard."

He growled in annoyance and pinned her wrist to her lower back.

"Of course it's hard. I'm not spanking you for kicks, Alice. It's *supposed* to hurt. It's *supposed* to make you think the next time you have the urge to light up a cigarette or jeopardize your safety in some other stupid, bratty way, 'Am I really ready to break the rules? Do I really wanna feel that pain again? Do I really wanna make my daddy angry?'"

A quiver of fear and longing turned her stomach. This wasn't what she'd expected! His palm fell again and again, until her flesh was hot and throbbing and her eyes were filled with tears.

"You messed up today, Alice," he said again, releasing her wrist, and bringing both of his hands down to massage her sore bottom.

Alice took a deep shuddering breath. "Yes, Daddy," she sobbed.

Her voice was husky and soft in the sudden stillness of the room, and it seemed to make his own voice deepen in response.

"Explain to me what you did that was wrong." His tone was as hard and unyielding as his palm.

"I-I went outside and smoked a cigarette," she admitted. "It was a dumb thing to do."

"Dumb, yeah. Because you have friends who love you, a kid who adores you, and you need to do everything you can to keep yourself healthy," he told her. "Everyone has vices, baby. But you smoke that shit because you're having one bad day, because something inside you is craving attention, and you're playing Russian roulette, yeah? Not just with your life, but your kid's future."

She inhaled sharply. God, when he said it like that… It was pretty fucking selfish. "You're right," she said, her shoulders sagging slightly. "I'm sorry." And this time it wasn't a line. She truly meant it.

Slay nodded against her shoulder, and his massaging hands turned teasing, rubbing her in wider and wider circles, getting closer to her pussy and then finally dipping beneath the edge of her thong.

Alice sucked in a breath.

So did Slay. "Jesus… All this for me, Allie-girl?" he breathed, moving his fingers through the wetness he found there.

Allie-girl. Something about that simple nickname made her heart stutter. No one had ever given her a nickname before. She'd always been Alice, sweet and wholesome and dependable. But Allie-girl… She sounded fun and lighthearted. Cared for. Loved.

And then Alice stopped thinking because his fingers started moving with more deliberation, stroking up and down her slit in an almost teasing way, strumming around her clit without ever quite touching. She arched her back, pushing her fingers against his hand.

"Yeah, like that, baby doll," Slay encouraged. "Fuck, yes. Just like that. Take what you need from Daddy."

With a light, delicate touch that nearly made her lose her mind, he stroked her while she quivered and writhed, wordlessly begging him for more. She couldn't believe how hearing him call himself Daddy was amping her up. The pleasure built and built until it became almost painful. She pushed herself to her tiptoes, trying to get more from him, desperate to come. And when she was sure she couldn't take it even one second longer, he moved his finger in a single, firm flick and she exploded, her entire body pulsing with the force of her orgasm.

She had never come so hard in her life, and he'd barely touched her.

But even as she panted and struggled to bring her brain back online, she felt his breath on the back of her neck and knew she needed more from him, more connection, more pleasure, more, more, *more.*

"Slay, please," she begged, arching and writhing. This man stole her wits, stole her words.

"You want Daddy's fingers?" he taunted, plunging two fingers inside her. "Hmmm?"

"Nooo! Sl—*Daddy*…" She was panting. God, it felt amazing. But still, she needed more.

"Say it," he demanded roughly, his own voice tight with need. "Tell me what you want. Tell me *who* you want."

"I want *you.* Please, Daddy!"

She felt his fingers disappear and heard him release his zipper with a harsh groan that made her heart speed impossibly faster. She dimly heard the rustle of his jeans as they dropped to his ankles, the crinkle of the condom wrapper as he tore it open, but she couldn't concentrate on any of it.

"Hurry," she begged.

And just a second later, he was lined up against her, pulling her thong to one side, ready to push inside her.

Just like she had earlier, right before he'd spanked her, she felt a burst of anticipation so keen it was nearly torture. But then it was replaced by a sensation of overwhelming rightness. Life would be forever divided into all the moments before this, and then all the moments after, and it was always meant to be so.

And then Slay was pushing himself into her fully and she didn't think anymore.

Oh dear God.

In practically every romance novel she'd ever snuck home from the library as a kid, the innocent virginal heroine looked down at the hero's equipment with wide eyes and said something stupid like, "It's so big! I don't think it'll fit." Even as an inexperienced teenager, Alice had rolled her eyes because *duh*, biology! It was kinda *made* to fit. And as an experienced adult, she'd figured it was one more way that romance novels messed with a girl's expectations.

But apparently she hadn't been hanging out with the right guys, because right now *fitting* was actually kind of a concern. An excellent, excellent concern. The best problem she'd ever had.

"Shit," Slay said. "Fuck. Baby, you're so tight." His voice was harsh, almost angry, but he reached his hand around to stroke her clit again, making her relax, helping her to take him more easily.

The best response Alice could muster was, "Ungh."

"That's it. That's it, my girl. Daddy's good girl" he whispered.

Then she was arching, bending toward the wall, supporting herself with both forearms while Slay curled around her. While one of his hands was stroking her, the other was holding her hip as he moved against her, over and over and over again. Every stroke brought his pelvis against her, causing an answering ache in her sore bottom. He whispered filth and nonsense in her ear.

"My Alice is so fucking sweet."

"Take it, Allie-girl. Take all of me. That's it. Fuck, yeah, that's it."

"I pictured us just like this, how your pussy would milk my cock while your sweet mouth called me Daddy."

It was all too much.

Alice didn't come, she splintered. Fractured. Her vision went black, her ears stopped hearing, her body went completely still.

And when she came back to herself, minutes or hours or days later, her first thought was *Holy shit. The novels were right about that, too.*

Slay was breathing, panting in her ear. He'd paused, while she'd been turned inside out, and was stroking her back, waiting, still so, so hard inside her.

She arched back against him, encouraging him to move again, wanting him to feel the same thing she'd just felt.

He didn't need any more encouragement. His hips drew back and then thrust forward in a way that had nothing to do with practiced technique, but was primal and rough and perfect. He splayed his own massive hand next to hers on the wall, bracing himself, bracing them *both*. Within seconds, he was roaring in her ear, and she could feel him pulsing inside her, leaning his weight against her for a moment, just a moment, and trusting her to take it. So she did.

Then he was standing, dealing with the condom, pulling up his jeans, turning her around to face him, and sliding her skirt back into place.

She'd just had the most mind-blowing orgasm, and the single greatest moment of sexual connection ever... and she hadn't removed a single piece of her clothing.

Before she could even recover her breath, he was pulling her to him and lifting her chin with one finger, pressing a soft, sweet kiss to the corner of her mouth.

"Listen to me, Allie-girl. If you didn't get it when you walked in the room, you'd better get it now. Things have changed between us." His voice was deep and soft and oh-so-sure. "You follow my rules now. They're simple, but they are very, very serious. No risky behavior. No breaking Club rules. No lying or hiding shit from me. You do any of those things, I'll bare your ass again and show you what a *real* spanking feels like. Got it?"

"A *real* spanking?" she asked, feeling her eyes widen.

"Yeah, babe. This was a warm up," he scoffed. "Now tell me you get what I'm saying."

Once again, she wasn't sure she got it at all. But she nodded anyway. No risky behavior? Yeah. Fine.

He smirked and shook his head, and once again he replied, "You don't. But you will."

"You weren't even talking to me yesterday," she muttered inanely.

"Mmm," he agreed, stroking a finger over her cheekbone. "Thought that was the best thing for both of us, me keeping an eye on you from a distance. Thought you'd be safer that way. But now I realize you need me to keep a *closer* eye on you."

At his words, her brain shifted back into gear with a nearly audible *click*, and launched her from her sated stupor into a full-scale freak out. Someone to keep an eye on her? Like a body-guard? Like a babysitter? Who just also happened to have sex with her? Yeah, that wouldn't be weird or confusing at all.

And just how far did he think his power over her extended? It was fine for them to play a scene here or there—hell, she'd welcome it. Thanks to the spanking and the mind-blowing orgasm he'd given her, all the tension she'd been carrying for days had melted from her bones and she felt invigorated.

But beyond The Club, she didn't play the part of a submissive. She couldn't afford to. She had a family, a *son*, she had to be strong for, and an image to uphold for their sakes. She could imagine what the rich PTA bitches at Charlie's school would say if they knew she *worked* at The Club, let alone that she liked to play.

No, she needed to do what she should have done before she walked into this room—set some ground rules and some hard limits.

"I don't need a keeper, Slay," she protested, annoyed that her voice was still breathless, damn it.

Inside his pocket, his phone chirped.

"Babe, you still smell like cigarette smoke," he said wryly, as though this were all the explanation necessary.

He fished the phone from his pocket, looked at the display, and frowned. "Shit. They need me on the first floor. Come on, I'll walk you back to the bar."

Alice shook her head. "I need a minute," she said, gesturing towards the little bathroom. "Gotta clean up."

Translation: *Gotta process whatever the hell just happened.*

She'd wanted Slay. And she could admit that she'd maybe, *maybe* been unconsciously trying to get him to punish her tonight by acting out. In the moment, the daddy-thing had been hot. Kinky, yes, but in a way that felt natural and right.

Now though, it all seemed *off*. The weight of her child, her parents, her jobs, her *life*, settled back on her shoulders, reminding her that she didn't have time to play babygirl to a six-five tattooed bad boy. She had too many *adult* responsibilities to take care of.

Slay watched her face intently. Then his phone chirped again and he sighed.

He leaned forward and pressed a kiss to her forehead.

"Don't overthink this, Allie-girl," he told her gruffly. And then before she could protest, he shook his head and added, "I know you *will*, because you obsess about shit until down is up and right is left. But never mind. Daddy will sort you out."

Then with a wink—yes, Alex Slater could apparently wink—he turned and left the room, leaving Alice with wide eyes, a racing heart, and the feeling that, for a man so determined to keep her safe, Slay sure knew how to scare the crap out of her.

Chapter 2

Slay slammed the door of his massive black SUV and clicked the lock button on his key ring. The doors gave a satisfying *click* before he turned to his condo, gym bag slung over one shoulder and key ring in hand. His skin still glistened from the shower he'd taken after his workout as he took the steps three at a time. The adrenaline from his run and weight lifting was still pumping through him. It had nothing to do with what he'd done to Alice last night, right before he—nope. No, couldn't go there. He was getting a hard-on again just thinking about it, and he had shit to do.

"Why, if it isn't Alexander Slater," came a high, warbling voice as he opened the door to enter his building.

"Evening, Betty," he said, setting the gym bag down so he could snag the bag that teetered precariously in his elderly neighbor's hands. He gently scolded, "Did you go shopping again without me? What'd I tell you about that?"

"Oh, go on with you," Betty said. Her hands shook as she jiggled her keys in hand, trying to open the door. He waited. He could open the door in less time with the bag tucked under his arm, but she needed to know she could still do this. "I got my hair done and thought I'd stop and get a few things. Go look through the bag. I picked up some cookies for you."

He shook his head as he took the double-stuffed Oreos from the bag. She primped her gray curls, and her blue eyes, framed with thin lashes and a pattern of laugh lines, smiled at him. Eighty-five years old and as many pounds soaking wet, Betty was fiercely independent and stubborn. Slay watched out for her when he was home, took her shopping when she allowed it.

"Thanks, Betty," Slay said, tearing open the cookies and shoving three in his mouth. "You need a ride this weekend?" he asked around the crumbs. She could apparently afford the studio condo in his complex, but relied on public transportation or taxis to get around.

She shook her head. "Not this weekend. But if you come by later tomorrow night, I'm making lasagna." Her blue eyes twinkled from behind her glasses.

"Can't, Betty," he said. "Got a shift at The Club." He wouldn't tell her exactly what *The Club* stood for, and led her to believe he was just a bouncer. She didn't need to know he was a *flogger-wielding* bouncer and a dominant, with a contractual obligation to make sure no one in The Club hurt one another beyond the bylaws Master Blake had in place.

"One of these nights, you need to take me to The Club and buy me a drink," Betty said, wagging a finger over her shoulder as she took out the half-size carton of eggs and quart of milk, placing them in the fridge.

"You need help?" Slay asked, smothering a smile. "And I'll think about The Club."

Betty's head was deep in the fridge but he still heard her muffled voice before the door clicked shut. "I'm fine. I might be old, but I'm not dead! Buy me a drink!"

Slay snorted. Like *that* would happen. "Later, Betty."

He went back to the entryway door, grabbed his stuff, and headed to his apartment. He regretted ever telling Betty he worked at a club, and didn't want her asking questions. He kept his shit tight. He didn't like the idea of all the little old ladies at the hair salon Betty visited speculating about what kind of club he worked for if Betty opened her mouth. No one needed to know. Matteo, his former Marine brother and fellow tattoo artist at *Inked*, was the only one who even knew that he was a dominant at The Club.

When he opened the door to his apartment, he glanced appreciatively around. The cleaning lady had been by, and his place gleamed. He couldn't be bothered to do shit like mop or clean bathrooms, but he was happy to pay someone to do it. A note on the counter awaited him.

Much thanks for the big tip, Mr. Slay. His lips quirked a smile before he wadded the note up into a ball and tossed it into the trash. He hadn't seen his cleaning lady Carmela, a petite, middle-aged Filipino woman, in weeks. Carmela was a single mom with two college-aged kids, a hard worker who didn't ask questions. Those were essential qualities in someone who worked for Slay. He tipped her well. His only rule was that she not touch the locked spare room. The room was off limits. He explained to Carmela when she first started working for him that it was his "office," and "the work I do is highly confidential." His office was locked to most people, especially his younger sister Elena and his housecleaner. It *was* where he did his "work" ...of a certain type... and his work *was* totally confidential. Still, even though he trusted Carmela, he checked the spare room every time she'd been there.

He took his key ring from his pocket and slid it into the keyhole. It clicked open. He turned the doorknob, and entered. It was dark in the room, the shades pulled intentionally. He flicked on the light switch.

A dark wooden spanking bench gleamed in the overhead light, padded, with thick leather straps that would fit around the slender wrists he couldn't get out of his mind. The wrists he'd taken and pinned above her head as he'd spanked her ass as she'd called him *Daddy*.

Alexander Slater was an experienced dominant. He'd spent years as a guard at Club Black Box, but after shit went down there, had recently taken on a full-time position as dungeon master at The Club. He liked Blake, and he sure as hell liked the people who worked at The Club. He'd seen it all and *thought* he'd experienced it all. But up until Alice, he'd only ever fantasized about any girl calling him Daddy. Hearing the words come out of Alice's mouth was unlike anything he'd ever fucking imagined.

He shook his head. Had to clear his mind. Walking over to the bench, he ran a hand along the polished finish, inhaling the scent. The mere smell of leather got him going, and his pants tightened, his cock straining as he envisioned Alice stretched across that bench. It was custom made, crafted from the highest quality cherry wood by one of Matteo's friends.

But Slay had never used it, nor any of the equipment currently in the room. He'd been waiting for Alice.

He'd been patient. He'd been waiting for the right woman, the one willing to play along with his kink and call him Daddy. He'd spent months watching her, testing her, seeing if she had the mettle to deal with his brand of kink. Now, he was taking off the gloves. Now he fucking itched to play with the toys he'd been handpicking.

To the right, he'd installed a post with pegs, perfect for tying the ends of the light restraints he favored. And next to that lay the chest which housed a small handful of implements—a thick leather strap, a thinner but wicked leather tawse, and a riding crop, among other things. He'd owned a wooden paddle and on occasion applied it with the last girl he'd dated, but she hadn't been into the way he liked to do things. She'd *laughed* at him when he'd finally told her his daddy fantasy, and he'd spanked her for her disrespect. But he didn't get through to her, partly because he hadn't felt comfortable spanking for disrespect, when clearly, the daddy thing wasn't her deal. They'd moved on, and he hadn't brought it up with any other girl because it never felt quite right. He fingered the new leather paddle that had a good heft to it. It would be sensual but pack a lasting bite. Lifting the strap, he stroked the smooth leather in his hand, imagining what it would be like to tie Alice's pretty little wrists to the pole, and stripe that gorgeous ass while she begged him.

Please, Daddy.

Yes, Daddy!

I'm sorry, Daddy!

He closed his eyes briefly, growing heady with excitement at the possibility. She'd give him oh so many reasons to spank her. He swallowed, placing the strap back down.

His eyes glanced to the other side of the room, where another locked door led to a walk-in closet that housed another secret, another aspect of his life. Even Alice wouldn't be allowed in there.

He'd been watching Alice for a good long time now, and she didn't even know it. He'd put her to the test, and time and again, she'd passed those tests she didn't know she was taking. It was better that way.

Could she really obey? Was she able to withstand being denied what she wanted?

Was she in it for the kink or did she want something *more?*

Some would argue it hadn't been fair, what he'd done. He'd had his reasons. Entering into a full-time Dominant/submissive relationship with a woman was something he would never do blindly ever again. It took planning and forethought.

Alexander Slater was a patient man. He could wait for years for what he wanted.

But he was tenacious, a veritable pitbull. Once he bit, he didn't let go.

Slay shut and locked the door to his office, and pocketed the key. Opening the fridge, he grabbed a gallon of milk, and poured himself a glass. Glancing at the clock, he realized why he was so hungry. It'd been hours since lunch, and the workout had kicked his ass. His phone buzzed. Momentarily hopeful, he picked it up quickly. Disappointment sunk in when he saw it was Matteo, not who he'd hoped it would be.

Blake wants me and you to work out details on some shit with the new room they're renovating. You game to meet at Cara?

Cara was Matteo's younger brother Tony's Italian restaurant, and Slay didn't have to be asked twice.

On my way, he responded. But before he pocketed his phone, he sent another message.

Behaving yourself, Allie-girl? He sent it, smirking at the phone. After the good spanking he'd given her earlier, the reminder to behave would likely have her squirming. But if he were honest, he really did want to make sure she was behaving. No more smoking, or doing dangerous shit. Her response came back immediately.

Yep. I'm being a good girl. No more smokes, came home after work, and even ate my veggies.

He smiled as he responded. *Shift at The Club tonight?* She sometimes worked a double, and he couldn't remember what shift she had.

Not tonight. Nodding, he wondered if she'd be game for coming and grabbing a bite with him at *Cara.*

Want to get some food with me at Cara? Charlie can come. I can get you guys some dessert. There's room in my truck. He snickered. He could fit most of Charlie's kindergarten class in his truck. But his phone lay silent, no response from her. He frowned, wondering what was going on, but reasoned she was a busy mom and couldn't exactly have an on-the-spot text convo to suit his whims. Another message beeped in, but it was a work-related message which he glanced at and moved on. He had shit to do, but not now. His jaw grew tight and he tapped his foot.

Some would say he'd been stringing her along for a while now. He wished he could forget the look of hurt and betrayal on her face when he'd sent her packing after she'd visited him in the hospital. It was better for her not to know some things, at least now. And eventually, she'd come to see that everything he'd done, *everything*, had been in her best interest all along. It would take time, but she'd see.

He'd held her at a distance. But now that she'd shown him what she was capable of, and what she really needed, things between little Allie and Slay were about to change. *Shit.*

Things were going to change.

His phone buzzed.

No, I think I'm going to have a quiet evening home tonight. He frowned, disappointed, but knew he had to respect her schedule, wishes, and comfort zone.

Ok, babe. You be a good girl and call me before you go to bed tonight.

The response came a minute later.

Okay.

He looked sternly at his phone, as if it somehow knew what he expected and would hop to obey.

Try that again? You know how I asked you to respond.

He wondered how she was feeling on the other end. He would find out, eventually.

Okay, Slay.

He narrowed his eyes as he shot off another text. *That's ten, babe, with my hand, over my knee. One more time, or the next time we meet, you get the strap.*

He was playing hardball and he knew it, but shit was changing.

Yes, Daddy.

Warmth flooded his chest and his cock twitched. Fuck, he loved that shit.

Good girl.

When he arrived at *Cara*, Matteo hailed him down. Matteo was sitting next to Hillary, his arm strewn casually but protectively around her shoulders. Tessa Damon, the auburn-haired girl who'd hooked up with Tony and was the manager of *Cara*, sat next to Hillary. They were looking at something in a catalog and chattering away. Matteo gestured for Slay to pull up a chair.

"What's up, girls?" he asked them, giving Matteo a chin lift. "Matt."

Hillary, the pixie-like blonde Matteo had fallen head-over-heels for, smiled up at him. "We're trying to come up with some ideas for Nora for Christmas. You remember Nora?"

Slay stifled a snort. Was Hillary on crack? Like he'd forget the girl he'd teamed up with a brother to rescue from a drug-infested scene, not two months ago?

"Course I know Nora," he growled, earning him a narrowed-eyed look from Matteo and pursed lips from Tess, but Hillary's eyes just grew wide. Damn, he hadn't meant it to come out so harshly. But his arm still ached at times from the gunshot wound he'd sustained in that rescue. Shit these girls could get themselves into trouble.

"Nora's babysitting for Alice these days, we wanted to chat when she wasn't around. Then in the spring, we're thinking about having a graduation party for her. Looks like she might be graduating as valedictorian."

"You know what that means?" Matteo asked.

Slay rolled his eyes and flicked his wadded-up straw wrapper at Matteo. "Of course I know what it means. I'm not a dumbass, dumbass." He turned to Tess. "Nice. I'll be there. You all having it here?"

Tessa nodded. *Cara* had a nice, large function room. Slay also knew that Tony was pretty crazy about Tessa's little sister, Nora, and he'd want a top-notch party for her.

Nicole, one of the waitresses at *Cara*, came to the table. She looked suddenly shy, as if he were going to bite her. It was a look Slay was all too familiar with. He was a big guy, and he knew chicks dug that, but he also knew with his deep voice, muscles, and tats, he could be intimidating. He smiled at Nicole, scanning the menu. The special tonight was Tony's hand-rolled ravioli. His stomach rumbled. He placed his order, noting Nicole's hands shook slightly, but she looked flattered that he'd remembered her name. She scurried away

"When did Nora start sitting for Alice?" he asked, as he nabbed a roll, eating half of it in one bite and not even bothering with the butter.

Tessa picked up a roll and tore it open. "Oh, tonight's the first time," she said. "They've been talking about it for a while, but tonight was the first time Alice needed her."

Slay froze. Why would tonight be the first time, if Alice were staying home?

"Oh?" he asked, and his voice had dropped. He could tell by the way Hillary and Tessa shifted, and looked at each other, that he'd likely gotten scarier. "And where's Alice tonight?" he asked, trying his best to sound nonchalant and instead sounding like an inquisitor before a grand execution.

"I…" Tessa said, her voice trailing off.

Matteo, however, was not into pussy-footing around. "I think she's on a date," he said, tearing into the bread.

The roll sat like a rock in Slay's stomach. Yeah, he hadn't exactly asked Alice to be his girlfriend and to be exclusive. But hadn't he made it clear that lying wouldn't be tolerated?

"A date," he growled, a statement, not a question.

Hillary's cheeks had flushed, but Tessa looked him straight in the eye. "Yes, a *date*. Does this bother you, Slay? I seem to recall her telling me how you dismissed her from the hospital when she came to visit."

He clenched his jaw, looking her back straight in the eye, as he pointed a finger at her. "There are some things you don't know about, and should stay out of." He liked Tessa, but the girl needed to mind her own fucking business.

"Maybe it *is* my business if a guy plays with my friend," she said. "Drops her like a hot potato when she'd do anything for him, then gets all controlling and shit when he finds out she's on a date."

Seriously?

He dropped his voice low as he leaned across the table and spoke in his most dom-like way. "That's enough."

Tessa's cheeks flushed a little, and though she still met his eyes, she squirmed a bit. Good. Slay continued. "I've got my reasons for the way things went down. I'll admit, I fucked up. That doesn't mean it's okay for her to lie to me. If Alice lied to you, I don't think we'd be sitting here having this conversation, now would we?"

"Lied?" Tessa asked. She blinked.

"Yeah, *lied*," he said. "But you don't worry about that. I can handle this." And with that, he got to his feet. "Any idea where she went on a date?"

Tessa shook her head, along with Hillary.

"Careful, brother," was Matteo's only admonition, as Slay lifted his hand and left.

He'd find her. And when he did, she'd know that Alexander Slater—her *daddy*—was not a man who fucking played around.

———

He dialed the first number on his speed dial as he fired up his truck, waiting for the response. He wanted to give her a chance to talk before he went to Plan B. Not surprisingly, her phone went to voicemail.

He dialed the second number on speed dial.

"Hey, man," came the answer.

Slay responded without introduction. "She lied to me. Told me she was having a quiet night in."

Swearing on the other end of the line. "She lied to you, all right. Was just gonna message you. Yeah. She isn't home. She's out with a guy. Wanted to run his specs before we contacted you, so we could give you full intel."

Slay gritted his teeth, wishing he had a fucking address already. If she even knew half the shit that was going down…

"You're not gonna like this, brother."

He closed his eyes briefly before growling back into the phone. "Fucking spill."

"She's with a guy named Gary Levitz. Skinny guy, filthy rich, goes to her parents' church. Mom and dad set her up, looks like."

He nodded. "Go on."

"Our sources say this guy is tight with Salazar. Inner circle, man. Bad news."

Slay pulled the phone away from his ear and swore, his eyes shut momentarily before he returned to the phone.

"Where?" he asked.

"Not far from *Cara*. I'll give you the address."

Seconds later, he was peeling out of the parking lot of *Cara* trying to quell his rising temper.

At one point, he'd considered telling Alice everything—all about the surveillance equipment hidden in the room beyond his playroom, about the hand-picked crew of former soldiers he worked with for more than a year as they investigated and infiltrated Chalo Salazar's cartel. He'd wanted no secrets between them.

But as quickly as he'd had the thought, he'd dismissed it. He had men on the inside whose lives depended on maintaining secrecy. And the less Alice knew about the twisted, demented shit a flesh-and-drug peddler like Salazar was up to, the happier and safer she'd be.

Still, this meant he needed Alice to obey him without hesitation. And he'd make it loud and clear that Alice was *his*.

He didn't know which he wanted to do first—kick Levitz for trying to date his girl, or spank Alice's little ass until she couldn't sit for a week.

Chapter 3

"So that creates a situation, a 'perfect storm,' if you will, where *we*, that is to say, Marlborough Investment Group, can step in and really set our own terms, you know? Which is how we've grown into the worldwide leader in such a short time. But what really sets us apart…"

Alice smiled and nodded politely at the man on the other side of the table. Her mind was buzzing with a thousand thoughts—the supplies she needed to buy for Charlie's school project, how to make the landlord come and fix the kitchen faucet that had suddenly started shooting water like a geyser, why her car was making a *tick-tick-tick* noise and how much it would cost to repair. Not one of her thoughts was related to whatever the hell her date was droning on about.

Her *date*.

Gary Something-or-other. A successful, upstanding pillar of the community, who ran an outreach program for troubled teens at her parents' church. "He'd be wonderful for you and Charlie! Give him a chance!" her mom had pleaded. And she'd agreed, because a man like Gary was exactly what she needed. Steady. Dependable. The kind of guy who would fix her kitchen sink in two seconds (or, okay, more likely *pay someone else* to fix it, but Alice wasn't picky). The kind of guy who was just begging for a six-year-old to present him with a hand-painted "Number One Dad" mug on Father's Day. Not like some people, who only wanted to *play* at being a—

Nope, don't go there.

But it was hard not to make comparisons, considering the man in front of her was the anti-Slay. He had not a single piercing, not the barest hint of a tattoo. He was thin, but still rounded-looking, with a broad, pale face, pink cheeks, and a cap of golden hair—like a Botticelli angel, only skinnier. His shoes and suit probably cost what Alice made in a month. And when he'd arrived at the restaurant she'd chosen, a nondescript Italian place in a strip mall not far from her house, and he'd rushed over to greet her with a beaming smile and effusive apologies for being a few minutes late, she couldn't help but notice that even in her lowest heels, the man's eyes were barely at the same level as her own.

She tried to force her mind to focus on whatever the hell Gary was talking about. She vaguely recalled asking him what he did for a living… like, ten minutes ago. And he was obviously extremely excited about what he was saying. She couldn't recall the last time she'd been so excited.

You were excited last night, a little voice in her mind whispered.

No. Nope. Not. Going. There.

After a moment, Gary's speech wound down. He gave a little half-shrug, as though embarrassed that he'd gone on so long, and Alice felt a pang of shame. *This* was the kind of guy she *wanted*—sweet and reliable. It wasn't right that she should be thinking of anyone else while they were on their date.

She gave him her most engaging grin. "Wow! That is so impressive!" She was certain that she *would* have been impressed, had she paid attention.

He smiled broadly at her compliment. "So tell me about *you*,

Alice. Do you work… *here*?" He cast his eyes around the room, at the sparkling Christmas lights that blinked in the front window and the tired carpet on the floor. "Your mom said you're a… waitress?"

Alice paused. Was she imagining that slight hesitation before he said the word *waitress*, as though he was hoping she'd correct him? Maybe tell him she was a wealthy undercover philanthropist instead? Sorry, Gary. No such luck.

"Uh, yeah. I'm a waitress, but I don't work here. I work at an Italian restaurant. *Cara*. In the North End," she replied. She hesitated, and decided that she wouldn't mention a thing about The Club. Not right away. If he was hesitant about her being a waitress, he might be totally scandalized if he knew she worked at a BDSM club.

Then how will he react when you tell him you like to be spanked, *Allie-girl?* The taunting voice in her head sounded remarkably like Slay now, and she ruthlessly ignored it.

Gary nodded enthusiastically. "I think I've heard of it," he told her. "But what's your ultimate plan?"

Alice frowned. "What do you mean?"

"I mean, when you get a *real* job, what do you want to do?" he elaborated.

A *real* job. *Ouch*. He wasn't the first person who acted like waitressing wasn't a real job, never mind that she worked harder than most of the people she knew, or that it enabled her to provide for her son. Yeah, it wasn't glamorous, but it was good, honest work.

Still, Alice hid the sting behind a smile and gave him the benefit of the doubt. Gary seemed like an ambitious guy. He'd probably expect that everyone was as ambitious as he was.

She fought the urge to tell him that she had taken college classes in criminal justice, that she'd ultimately wanted to pursue a career in law. But she'd traded that dream for the reality of giving her son the very best life she could. *And you don't need to justify yourself to anyone. You don't owe anyone an explanation*, she reminded herself. *Not to this guy, and not to…*

Her phone, which she'd placed face-down on the table, started to chime, saving her from replying to Gary.

"Excuse me," she told him as she flipped the phone over. "It's my babysitter."

Alice typed off a quick reply to Nora—*Sure, he can have ice cream*. But as she started to set the phone down again, her eyes snagged on her earlier text conversation and her pulse began to race with remembered excitement—and not a small amount of anxiety—as she scrolled through the texts.

Slay's messages had started coming in just before she left on her date this evening, almost as though he were omniscient or could sense a disturbance in The Force. She wouldn't put it past him. *Behaving yourself, Allie-girl?*

And damn, but that simple text message had made her heart squeeze, both then and now. Maybe because she could picture the cocky smirk on Slay's face as he sent it. Or maybe because just thinking about him made the soreness in her bottom, which had been negligible all day, suddenly flare to life like he'd just spanked her again.

She knew that *not* responding would only encourage him, so she'd typed out a quick message as she'd sat in her car. *Yep. I'm being a good girl. No more smokes, came home after work, and even ate my veggies.*

It was true, she reminded herself. She simply didn't add that she'd left home again later. She also didn't share that hadn't felt any need to smoke, given that the spanking and sex last night had left her completely boneless and stress-free.

The man's ego was healthy enough already.

His response had been almost immediate. *Shift at The Club tonight?*

Alice had hesitated before replying. She hadn't wanted to mention her date with Gary, not that it was any of Slay's business anyway. Still, she'd sent a simple *Not tonight*, and prayed he'd drop it.

But he hadn't. Naturally. With his mind-reading instincts, he'd somehow known that there was more going on and he'd invited her out for dinner. For *dessert*. To let Charlie ride in his *truck*.

Alice's heart gave a quick pang of misgiving. Why had the man had to go and be sweet about it? She could just picture how Charlie's eyes would light up at getting to sit in Slay's big truck. But that would be just a one-time thing, wouldn't it? And it wouldn't do for Charlie to get used to that, to start to expect it. It wouldn't do for *her* to expect it either. By next week or next month or, heck, by *tomorrow*, Slay could've changed his mind right back again, and reverted to ignoring her.

So she'd held her breath, ignored her beating heart, and told him she planned a quiet evening at home instead.

Which wasn't a lie, right? She'd be home later and have a quiet evening after that. And she had been doing what she needed to do to protect herself and her kid.

"Everything okay?"

Alice guiltily glanced up from her phone at the man across from her, who watched her with sharp eyes and a slight frown. She'd been ignoring him.

"Er, fine," she said. "Just a… work issue."

"A work issue," Gary muttered, "I had no idea waitresses had to be on call."

Alice took a deep breath, mentally cursing Gary for his jerky comment. But her phone drew her gaze back like a magnet, and she scrolled further down.

That's ten, babe, with my hand, over my knee. One more time, or the next time we meet, you get the strap.

Yes, Daddy.

She felt her thighs clench and her belly flip in longing.

She shot a glance at Gary, who had cast his eyes to the ceiling and was pointedly (and, she thought, rather passive-aggressively) tapping his fingers on the table top, and gave a mental sigh. Now was not the time to dwell on Alexander Slater and his high-handedness… nor the way that high-handedness seemed to work for her in a major way.

Still, she could feel heat flood her cheeks when she read his final message. *Good girl.*

It's not real. It's a game to him, she reminded herself. *Reality is right in front of you.*

Taking a deep breath, Alice put down her phone.

———

"But honestly, *Pedro's* served me the worst margarita I've ever had in my life," Gary said with a shake of his head as he scooped up one last forkful of pasta. "I told the bartender, 'I'm all for the authentic Mexican experience. I mean, I've *been* to Cabo San Lucas. But I want the sand *under my feet*, not in my glass.' " He chuckled at his own joke.

Alice attempted something like a smile, but it was a chore to get her muscles to move in the proper way. There were so many things wrong with the shit coming out of this guy's mouth, she wasn't sure where to begin. And she knew, based on her attempts to address the homophobic things he'd said during the salad course and the elitist bullshit he'd spewed before their pasta arrived, that he wouldn't listen to a word she said anyway. This date was turning out to be a one-man show.

Which begged the question, of course, why she didn't just get up and leave. If it had been *Slay* saying such awful things, she'd have leapt up and read him the riot act before marching out the door, no matter how many spankings he threatened her with. But with Douchebag Gary, she'd held her tongue and kept the peace. Why was it easier to be herself with Slay?

Why did she instinctively know that Slay would never say such nasty stuff in the first place?

Mom and Dad love Gary, she reminded herself. *He's a good person. He has a successful career. He goes to church. He's dependable.*

But the thought of him airing his opinions in Charlie's hearing turned her stomach, and that's when she couldn't pretend to herself anymore. Charlie needed dependable; he didn't need a dependable *asshole*. She would be polite and she wouldn't make a scene, but she couldn't date someone like Gary, no matter how perfect he seemed on paper.

She toyed with her pasta—some spaghetti carbonara dish that couldn't hold a candle to the version Tony prepared at *Cara*—and then resolutely set her fork on the side of her plate with a clink.

"This has been a lovely evening," she began.

Gary nodded and signaled to the waiter, who came over to clear their plates and ask if they'd like dessert.

"No!" Alice said loudly. In a softer voice, she repeated, "Er, no, thank you. I really should be getting home."

The waiter, who had likely overheard just a little too much of Gary's diatribes, shot her a sympathetic glance. "All right then," he said. "I'll just bring over the…"

"I'll have the tiramisu and a coffee with amaretto," Gary said, as though he hadn't heard either of them. "She'll have the same."

Alice and the waiter exchanged a glance, and Alice lost her hold on her patience. "I don't *want* tiramisu," she said clearly, feeling her ears turn red as she rose to her feet. "Or coffee. In fact, I really need to be going…"

And then a deep voice came from behind her, a musky, smoky scent surrounded her, and she knew she was screwed.

"What's your hurry, *Allie-girl*?"

A large hand clamped on her shoulder and gently pushed her back down. In one smooth move, Slay snagged an empty chair from a nearby table and placed it between her seat and Gary's. Then he sat down, straddling it, folded his enormous tattooed forearms along the top of the chair back, and glanced from her to Gary with what seemed to be avid curiosity… if you couldn't feel the absolute fury that pulsed beneath his skin. Alice could definitely, *definitely* feel it.

She shivered.

"So, what are we talking about, kids?"

Gary looked at Slay, and then at Alice, wordlessly demanding an explanation.

Good luck, Gary. I can't explain it either, she thought furiously. What the *hell* was Slay doing here?

"Gary, this is Slay—er, *Alex*," she corrected. "He's a… coworker."

Gary blinked. "You? Are a waiter?" he asked Slay, his gaze raking Slay from his shaved head, over his pierced ears and eyebrows, to the tattoos peeking over the top of his t-shirt and scrolling down both arms, and finally taking in the breadth of his muscular chest.

Slay gave him a smile that was anything but friendly. "Do I look like a waiter, Gary? Ask yourself, really look deep inside yourself, and think about it before you speak. Do I *look* like a waiter?"

Gary's eyes widened. "No," he whispered. "You look like a…"

Slay's eyes narrowed, and his smile turned feral, daring Gary to finish the sentence. "Like a *what*, Gary?"

Alice held her breath and waited to hear what insulting thing Douchebag Gary would say. A thug? A criminal? *I'll kick him in the balls*, she thought. And then blinked in shock at her instinctive need to defend Slay, even when he was being a total jerk.

But douchebag though he might be, Gary wasn't a total idiot. "Like a *manager*," he squeaked diplomatically.

Slay snickered and his eyes glinted with real humor. "There

ya go!" He reached out one broad palm the size of Gary's head, and clapped Gary on the shoulder in a friendly way that would likely leave a bruise. "You might just make it out of this in one piece."

Slay's voice was so pleasant that it took a minute for the meaning of his words to penetrate. Alice knew the second the threat registered, because Gary's eyes narrowed. "I don't think you know who I am," Gary blustered.

Slay smiled his not-friendly smile again. "Funny you should say that, Gary, funny you should say that. Because that's what first dates are all about, isn't it? Getting to know each other?"

Slay turned to look at Alice fully for the first time. His brown eyes were nearly glowing with anger, but it was the hurt she glimpsed there, the betrayal, that made her catch her breath. Guilt churned in her stomach.

Slay continued, "I'd love to help you two along with that. Help you *break the ice*, see if there's a real *connection* here. You see, Gary, I know a few key things about Alice that I think you should be aware of."

Alice shook her head wildly, but Slay continued. "Like, did you know that our Alice is turning out to be a compulsive liar?"

Guilt turned to anger in her belly. "Slay, I am *not!*" she exclaimed.

Gary looked from her to Slay in confusion. "What are you talking about?"

"Well, *first*, she was caught smoking a cigarette after she said she didn't smoke," Slay explained, his eyes locked on Alice's. "But her daddy already made it *very* clear that he doesn't find that behavior acceptable, didn't he, honey?"

Her breath caught in her throat. Oh, God, it was so wrong. She wanted to kill him, absolutely *slaughter* him… and yet his words made her thighs press together and her clit pulse.

Slay looked at her expectantly. "I said, '*Didn't he, honey?*'" he demanded.

Alice sucked in a shaking breath. "He did," she agreed. Anything to get him to stop before he said something worse, something that would get back to her parents. "Please, Slay, don't…"

"And then tonight, she *lied* to her daddy," Slay continued in that same confiding tone. "Told him she was going to be staying *in* for the night when she was out on a *date*." Slay made a tsk-ing noise. "She'll answer for that, too, though, Gary, believe me. Her daddy is *none. too. pleased*."

Alice sucked in a sharp breath.

Gary shook his head. "That's ridiculous. I know Miss Cavanaugh's father, and he's well aware that I'm taking his daughter out tonight. He gave me his blessing."

Slay turned his focus to Gary. "Did he? Really? Hmm… I wonder. Because there are a few things I know about *you*, Gary, that I think *Alice* here should be aware of. And some things about your boss, too."

Gary's face flushed. "I think it's time for you to leave," he sputtered.

"Nah! Not when we're just getting acquainted!" Slay disagreed. "Tell me, how's Chalo doing?"

Gary's face bled of color. "What?" he whispered.

Slay held his gaze and said nothing for a moment. Then turning to Alice, he explained, "Your friend Gary has some very questionable work associates, Allie. Not all of them are endorsed by the Chamber of Commerce."

Alice looked at Gary, who looked back and forth between her and Slay with a look of mingled fear and outrage.

Huh. Maybe Gary's job at Marlborough Investment Group wasn't quite as boring as Alice had imagined. She suddenly wished she'd paid closer attention.

"That's crazy!" Gary cried.

"True enough, man, true enough. The things I've seen your boss do to people who cross him are truly crazy," Slay agreed, his voice sharp as a blade. "Shoulda read the fine print before you signed on to be his lapdog."

Alice felt her eyebrows rise. How the heck did Slay know Gary's boss?

"So here's how this is going to work," Slay said. His words were hard, no longer maintaining a pretense of affability now that his cards were on the table. "You're gonna walk out of this place right now with a smile on your face, and let me pay for your dinner. You'll go home and tell everyone that Alice, here, is a lovely and charming lady, but things just didn't work out. And then you'll forget that you ever knew her. You will lose her number. You will strike her name from your vocabulary. Understood?"

Gary appeared to be seething with anger and it was clear he wanted to argue, but couldn't. "Fine," he spat. Then he made as if to rise, but Slay put his hand on Gary's shoulder once more and held him down.

"Oh, one more thing you need to know about Alice before you go, Gary. She's *mine*. You need to get that, absorb it way down deep in every pore, and then pass the message along to all your, uh, *colleagues*. Anyone who breathes too close to her loses teeth, anyone who talks to her loses fingers, anyone who lays a hand on her loses more than that. Yeah?"

Gary looked Slay in the eye and what he saw there made him swallow. *Hard*. "Yeah," he agreed sourly. Then he stood up and looked at Alice. "Lovely evening," he said. He walked away muttering, "*Fuck*."

Alice stared after him as he left, trying to get a handle on her emotions. What the *hell* had just happened? She felt outrage at Slay, some measure of guilt she was pretty sure was misplaced for not keeping him informed about her every movement, anger at Gary for being a douchebag, and disappointment in herself, both for agreeing to this clusterfuck of a date in the first place and then for not walking away an hour ago. And beneath it all, a warmer, deeper emotion that she didn't want to acknowledge. Slay had rescued her. He cared.

Slay stood too. He reached for his wallet and threw a bunch of cash on the table, then grabbed her elbow and yanked her up. "Let's go, Alice."

She grabbed her coat and purse, and allowed him to steer her out of the restaurant without causing a scene, but when they reached the parking lot, she shrugged out of his grasp.

"Let me go, Slay. You're hurting me."

He wasn't, not really, but she had no desire to talk to him right now. She needed to get home, calm down, make sense of what had happened before she discussed this.

She tried to stalk to her car.

He whirled her around to face him.

They were alone in the parking lot, but for a few empty cars. The cold air made Slay's breath fog, and she could see his chest heaving as he fought to calm himself.

"What the *fuck* was that?" he demanded.

Fine. He wanted to have it out here, in a public parking lot, before she'd gotten a handle on herself?

She took a step closer and let her own fury loose.

"That was *you* being a total *ass*!" she cried.

"Me! You're cheating on me with that… that… Jesus, Alice, I can't even think of a word to describe him… and you think *I'm* being an ass?"

She threw out her hand. "You can't *cheat* on someone if you're not *together*, Slay!"

"Not together? Not *together*? You called me *Daddy*, Alice. You've been in the scene long enough, babe. You know what that means."

She shook her head violently in denial. "No! There's where you're wrong! I have no *fucking idea* what it means! You ignore me for months, *months!* You reject me time and again. And then suddenly, you change your mind and come after me. You——" She

47

broke off, glancing around to make sure they were still alone before lowering her voice to a harsh whisper. "You spank me, you fuck me against a wall, you make me call you *Daddy* while we're having sex, and just like that I'm, *what*? Your submissive? *You've* been in the scene long enough, *babe. You* know it doesn't work like that."

She saw his jaw work back and forth while he absorbed this. Somewhere in the distance, a car alarm sounded, then shut off. The cold air slowly froze her cheeks and her fingers as they stared at one another.

"You lied," he said eventually, calmer now.

She looked into his eyes, barely visible in the glow of the streetlight. Once again, she saw that below the anger was hurt, and she realized her mistake.

All along, she'd thought the daddy thing was just part of the kink, part of the sex, and she'd been going along with it, but telling herself it wasn't real. That it would end as soon as he got tired of sleeping with her. But what if… what if he *was* being real? What if he really had intended to be her dominant, her daddy, long-term? That would mean that *she* had unknowingly been the one messing with *him*.

Damn.

She sucked in a breath and blew it out. "Yeah. I lied. I shouldn't have done that."

"You shouldn't have been out with him to begin with," he said angrily. "And let me be clear. I don't want you to see that fucker, not even to *talk* to him. If you see him hanging around for whatever reason, if he calls you, texts you, emails you, sends you a freakin' telegram, you tell me immediately, and I'll make sure he gets the message to go away, you get me?"

She shook her head. "Slay, I have no idea what's happening here," she said honestly. "Straight talk right now, okay? Total truth?"

He nodded once, shortly, and she continued, "I don't know

what you want from me beyond sex, and I'm not sure if this whole thing," she gestured between them, "is right for me. For *Charlie*. For the record, I'd already figured out that Gary was an asshole, but I had no idea just how…"

She stopped as a thought occurred to her, chilled her far more than the cold night could.

"Slay?" she asked slowly. "How did you know where I was tonight?"

Nora and Tessa knew she was on a date, and, therefore, the whole crew likely knew. But no one but Gary knew the restaurant she'd chosen, and she doubted that Gary had confided in Slay.

"I had a guy tailing you," Slay said. "A guy who does work with me, contract security work, has been watching you, protecting you, when I wasn't around. Turns out, it was a good thing he was."

She blinked and felt her jaw sag. He said it so matter-of-factly, like he wasn't dropping a verbal bomb right here in this parking lot, like he hadn't detoured so far into Wrongville he'd never find his way out.

When she couldn't summon words from beneath her anger and outrage, he continued. "You're *mine*, Alice."

As though that explained his actions? As though it justified them? The unmitigated arrogance of his statement jogged her words loose.

"Oh, yeah? I'm yours? Because *you* suddenly decided you want me? Well, isn't that *super?* Aren't I *lucky?* How about you get *this*, Alex Slater? Get it, you know, deep in your pores or whatever the fuck," she said, imitating the deep, threatening voice he'd used on Gary. "*I* haven't decided if I want *you* yet!"

He folded his arms across his chest, unperturbed by her anger. "Thought this was *straight talk*, Allie," he taunted. "*Total truth*. You want me. We both know it."

She shook her head. "I don't mean sexually, Slay."

"I don't either," he growled, stepping towards her. "You want me to be your dom. You know you do. And part of me being your dom is protecting you."

She bit back an instinctive denial. *Total truth*, she reminded herself.

"I want you to be my dom," she admitted, watching heat flare in his eyes. "But I don't know that you can give me what I need. I don't want to be watched or babysat. Doing creepy stalker shit without my knowledge or consent doesn't make me feel protected. It makes me feel threatened and coerced. *Weak*."

His head went back and his arms crossed over his chest.

"Believe me, I have enough people in my life who'd love to boss me around and control me," she continued, thinking of her parents, her neighbors, even some of her friends. "But I have a kid, Slay. I need to be strong. I need someone who'll help make me *stronger*. I need a partner, not someone who wants me to play a role when it's convenient for them."

"Is it so hard to believe that's what I want too?" he asked. "The real deal?" He stepped toward her and her heart pounded with hope and longing. "I've been waiting for this, for you, a long time. So, yeah, I was cautious, I took things slow. I waited, I watched you. I needed to be sure that you could give me what I needed, Allie. That it was what you needed, too. And now I'm sure. You're it for me."

You're it for me. She'd wanted to hear him say that for so long… But if he thought she'd melt at this statement, he was dead wrong.

"So… the past few months have been, what? A test?" she demanded. "To see if I was submissive enough, babygirl enough, to meet to your expectations?"

He set his jaw but didn't deny it.

"Slay, at any point in your thinking, did it occur to you that your sub, your babygirl, would have needs too?"

His eyes narrowed. "Christ, Allie. Don't be ridiculous. Of course it did. And that's why I'm trying…"

She shook her head and stepped forward, until they were nearly toe-to-toe.

"You're trying to give me what *you think I should need*. What some random stereotypical babygirl that you have in your mind should need. But what I *really* need is a different thing completely! I need for my opinions and feelings to be heard. I need someone who will put me and my kid first. Who's not just about spanking my ass in the middle of the night, but fixing my goddamn kitchen faucet, which is spraying hard enough to put my eye out! I don't need someone who insists I call him Daddy without doing a damn thing to *be* my daddy—like making me feel safe, like calming me down. You want the real deal? Then show me you can be that, Slay. And *then* we'll talk!" she said furiously.

He leaned down so that his face was inches from hers, his brown eyes no longer angry but assessing, and said a single word. "Fine."

"Fine?" she demanded. "Just like that?"

"Yeah, baby. Just like that," he agreed, his lip twitching up at the corner.

She shook her head. Arrogant, gorgeous man. "Slay, you need to *listen*," she repeated.

"Listened, Allie. Heard every single thing you said. You're right. I should've approached this differently. My error. I see that now."

She stared at him, almost unable to credit the words he was speaking. She hadn't been sure a man as completely and unapologetically dominant as Alex Slater *could* apologize without crumbling to dust, and yet here he was, admitting his error. Apologizing. *Well, more or less.*

His hand reached around to cup the back of her neck, his big fingers threading themselves through the long, blonde hair at her nape.

"Let me lay it out for you, babe. From this minute forward, let there be no doubt: I am your daddy." He cocked an eyebrow and Alice hesitated, then nodded minutely. He smiled. "The rules I put in place before still stand. But I'll add this one: From now on, you need to share with me. You need to tell me what you're thinking and how you're feeling. I'll listen. I'll sort you out. You'll trust me to take care of you and Charlie."

"Trusting can't be a *rule*, Slay," Alice whispered. "It's gonna take time for me to…"

He shook his head. "Trusting is a choice, Allie. Let me prove this to you. Give me that chance."

She wanted to! God, did she want to. A million doubts swirled inside her head—what were the chances that a man like Slay would want to take on the chores and challenges that came with a single mom and her kid?

But she'd be damned if she wouldn't give him the opportunity to try.

"Okay," she told him. "I'll trust you."

The hand in her hair tightened and she gasped.

"Say again?" he asked pointedly.

She blew out a breath and took a leap. "I'll trust you, *Daddy*."

His answering smile was breathtaking, and so was the fast, hard kiss he pressed to her lips.

"What time do you have to be home?" he demanded.

Her mind whirled to keep up. "Home? Uh, Nora's on until midnight," she stammered.

He glanced down at the large watch on his wrist. "That gives us nearly four hours," he told her, and his eyes, when he looked up at her, fairly smoldered. "Plenty of time."

"Time for what?" Alice asked, though the clench of her belly and the beading of her nipples meant that her body already had a pretty strong idea what he planned to do.

"Time to show little girls what happens when they lie to their daddies."

Oh. She swallowed and her palms became damp. Yeah, she definitely had enough time for that.

"Get in, Allie-girl," he said, cocking his head toward his enormous beast of a truck.

Alice didn't need to be told twice. Her heart was already thundering in her chest in anticipation of her imminent punishment.

"Yes, Daddy," she agreed.

Chapter 4

Y*es, Daddy.*

His cock tightened in his jeans. The image of Alice strewn over his lap and the *Yes, Daddy* dripping off her lips would make him lose his shit. God, this woman.

She tucked herself into the expansive, leather-clad interior of his truck as he swung himself up and shut the door. Clicking the lock, he leaned over and nabbed her seat belt, clicking it into place. She frowned slightly. "I can do my own seat belt."

He pursed his lips and raised his eyebrows. "Didn't say you couldn't," he muttered. "But now I am. There are a few things that make daddies a bit different from the rest, Allie-girl. And one of them means I get to take care of you. You want to establish trust? This is how we do it, baby. One little thing at a time. When your ass is in my truck, I drive, and I fasten your seat belt."

Her brows furrowed a bit, but she nodded. Good girl.

It would take some getting used to, but she'd learn.

He flicked his directional, taking a left on Main and tapping the steering wheel to the classic rock he always kept on low, as background music. He had a few choices. He could take her back to The Club, and easily find a room where he could punish her.

Or, he could take her back to his place and christen the "office" playroom.

The choice was an easy one.

"I'm taking you to my place," he said.

"Okay," she whispered. She kneaded her thighs with her hands, a nervous gesture. He barely tempered a smile. Good. She *ought* to be nervous. A babygirl about to get her ass punished had every reason to be nervous. Still, what she'd said back there at the restaurant, when she yelled at him...

Yelled at him.

He exhaled. The first thing she'd learn was that babygirls did not yell at their daddies.

But she'd made a good point. For months, as he'd waited her out, to see if she was really capable of being his full-time submissive, maybe it hadn't been the best idea to keep her in the dark. But if he *had* told her, would he have been able to truly see what she was made of? To see what she really *needed?*

Though he was a dominant who knew what he wanted and cowed to no one, he was not above a sincere apology. When he fucked up, he owned it. And he'd fucked up.

He reached a large hand out to her trembling hand on her thigh, and gently stopped the frantic kneading. "Baby."

He could hear her audible sigh as she stilled. "Yes?" she whispered.

"Being nervous before a discipline session is natural," he said. "But you're gonna hurt yourself pushing that hard. Hold my hand instead. Both hands in mine, honey." He placed his hand palm-up on her lap. She obediently put both hands in his, as he pulled onto his street. Closing his hand, he held hers still, his thumb circling the top of her hand soothingly. He could feel her visibly relax next to him. Good. Very good. One baby step at a time, and she would know. Eventually she would know he could be trusted.

He pulled into his parking lot and parked the truck.

"Wow, I didn't know you lived here," she said.

He shrugged. "Pretty decent neighborhood. People mind their own business, and the drive to work is easy." It took him ten minutes to get to The Club and fifteen to get to *Inked*. Rent here was steep, and she likely knew it, but both jobs paid well, and he could well afford it. He knew she could not, and felt it best to downplay that he could.

Alice moved to unfasten her seatbelt, and he barely stifled a chuckle. Oh, she had so much to learn, and it would be his pleasure to teach her. A low growl froze her in place.

"Daddy undoes your belt, honey. You keep your ass right there." He pointed a finger at her. Her hands stilled as she obeyed. He got down from his seat, slammed the door, and stalked over to her side. When he opened her door, it pleased him to see she hadn't moved. He unsnapped the seat belt and lifted her down from the cab. "A gentleman opens the door for you," he said low, in her ear, as he lowered her to the ground. "A daddy helps you out."

Her cheeks flushed and she lowered her eyes, nodding. Good girl. Such a very good girl. It was almost a shame he'd have to spank her ass.

Almost.

As they walked to the entryway of his apartment building, he reached a hand out to the back of her neck and gently grasped her. A claiming gesture, one that would make her know she was his and mark her. As they walked up the small stairway, he released her neck and held her hand, opening the door quickly and gesturing for her to enter the building first. "After you," he growled. It was an order, not a show of chivalry. She would soon see how things played out when she was in trouble.

As he led her in silence down the hall to his apartment, her wide eyes took everything in. He began to go over in his mind the reasons why he was going to make sure when little Allie went to bed tonight she'd be sleeping on her belly.

She'd lied to him. That fucking *douchebag jerk* she was with—God! She'd told him a flat out *lie*. There would be honesty between them no matter what.

She'd yelled at him. Called him an asshole. Disrespect, danger, dishonesty… he clenched his jaw, opened the door, and fairly hauled her in by the elbow. Her gorgeous eyes widened even further.

"Sit," he said, pointing to his sofa. He had shit to do before he dropped everything and focused on the session they were about to have. He wanted nothing on his mind but her when he had her over his knee.

"Wow, this place is…" she began, but he interrupted her.

"We're not here for chitchat, young lady," he growled. "There will be time for that *after*. For now, you sit your ass there until I call you to me." He had to temper his anger, and she needed to know he was serious. She needed a good, hard spanking. She needed to know what happened when she disobeyed him, and how seriously he took her safety. So much hung in the air between them.

It was imperative he get in touch with his men before another minute passed. He stalked to his office, opened the door and shut it firmly behind him. Walking to the second door, he opened it with a series of keys, input his pin, and pushed the door open. Time to unload intel, and make sure his guys were onto the sick bastard his girl had eaten dinner with. *God.*

He delivered his update in a clipped tone, and at the very end, called the men off. "She's with me for next few hours," he said. "You know the drill. When she's with me, you stay the hell away." Message delivered, he shut everything off. It had taken him all of three minutes to finish communications, before he shut and locked the door and went back into the main area of his "office."

Bringing her in here would likely scare the hell out of her. *Good.*

He stalked to the door, opened it up, and was prepared to call her into him. Having her come to him would work well, prepare her to submit to him and receive her punishment. And Christ, did she have one hell of a spanking coming.

But she wasn't sitting on the couch. For one brief minute, his heart leapt in his throat, as the very real threat Salazar and his gang posed weighed heavily on his mind. In two large strides, he was in the center of his living room, and there she was, not sitting *as she'd been told to do*, but standing in front of his entertainment center, staring at the small black and white picture of him and Matteo overseas.

"Wow," she said, "you guys look so *young*. It's almost cute how—"

"Alice." His voice was low, harsh, fucking *pissed off*.

She spun around to look at him, her eyes wide. "What?"

What? *God*, she wouldn't sit for a fucking *week*. He inhaled, slowly exhaling through his nose to calm his anger. When he spanked her, he needed to be in complete control of himself. He was so much bigger and so much stronger.

He spoke in a low, measured tone. "Where did I tell you to sit?" he asked.

Her eyes flitted to the couch and her mouth formed a perfect "o." "On the couch?" she whispered.

He realized he was clenching his jaw when he had to *unclench* it to speak. "Is that a question?"

She shook her head and swallowed hard. "Um, I… well, I *was* sitting, and then I saw this picture over here, and I…" her voice trailed off. "I should've stayed on the couch," she finished weakly.

He nodded. Her eyes dropped to his arms crossed on his chest, and she swallowed again, before she looked back up at him. Her voice was a whisper when she spoke. "I'm in big trouble, huh?" Her eyes looked both apprehensive, and something else… hopeful? He needed to spank her, he needed to spank her *hard*, and he needed to spank her *now*.

"Come here, please," he instructed. Folding her hands behind her back, she came to him, literally dragging her feet. Through the thin fabric of her top, he could see her peaked nipples. His cock tightened. She stood in front of him, craning her neck to look up into his eyes, and he stared back at her as he uncrossed his arms and placed one hand at her chin, her entire face engulfed in his large hand. He held her face so that her eyes didn't leave his.

"Yes, baby," he whispered. "You're in *big* trouble. Tonight, you'll learn that Daddy means what he says. Daddy needs to give you a good, hard spanking. Do you know that, Allie-girl?"

She swallowed, her eyes never leaving his. "Yes, Daddy," she whispered, her voice catching.

Though his palm itched to connect with her sweet, vulnerable ass, he was almost tempted to let her off the hook. She looked so sweet, *daddy* trailing off her lips like it was the most natural thing in the world.

He brushed a thumb over her cheekbone as he whispered to her. "I don't want to punish you. There are a million other things I'd rather be doing right now. But you need this." Her eyes watered as she nodded slowly.

His fingers traveling to the back of her neck, he pulled her closer to him and kissed her forehead. "No one's ever been in here," he said.

Pushing open the door, he felt her visibly tense with a sharp intake of breath as he drew her in the room. "Oh my God," she whispered. "Slay, you—I mean, Daddy—this is… holy hell. You have a dungeon in your apartment?"

"I prefer to call it my office," he said. "It's not exactly in the basement." He barely stifled a chuckle.

Her voice dropped as she turned to him. "No one's been in here?"

"No one, honey. You're the first." She smiled shyly. It was her room as much as it was his. But he'd ease her in. He watched with amusement as her wide eyes took everything in like a kid in a candy shop.

"There's a spanking bench. And… is that a tawse? Oh my God. I heard those are wicked. And… those are… *God!* Are you going to—those pegs, are those for you to—like, am I getting *whipped?* That's like, a whipping post, right? And there's… a flogger, and… oh, wow, a leather paddle… it's beautiful. But the acrylic one? Yeowch, no thank you." She continued, and he felt his lips quirk up. She was a connoisseur, and he had no small amount of pride as her wide eyes took everything in with a delightful mixture of awe and fear. It was cute, how she both admired his tools and rejected them.

As if she'd have a choice. So adorable.

She stilled as she approached the more hardcore toys in his collection. He'd been collecting for years. He was a patient man. Good things came to those who waited. It was his mantra.

She was fingering the Wartenberg wheel, the silky folds of a blindfold, and the thick adjustable cuffs. Her brows furrowed at the blindfold and her voice dropped. "Well, I'm disappointed," she muttered, her voice laced with sarcasm. "No St. Andrew's cross? Sensory deprivation hood? Ball gag?"

"I don't like gags," he said with a shrug. "If I want my girl's mouth gagged, I know how to gag it." Her eyes widened as he continued. "The cross is too removed. And I don't like hoods."

"Daddy?" she said softly, her eyes looking at him pleadingly. "I don't like blindfolds."

He nodded. "Understood." He'd respect her limits. He had to. But the freedom to explore his room was coming to an end.

"Alice. Eyes to me, now, babygirl." She looked over at him, her brows raised expectantly. He pulled out the straight-backed chair, the feet scraping along the floor. It was a large one, custom-made for his solid frame, big enough for him to easily take her over his lap, and sturdy enough to withstand a good, long session. "There will be time later for us to talk about what we like, what we don't, hard limits, and all that shit. For now, there's a certain little girl who needs a good session over her daddy's knee." His voice dropped. "Come here."

She swallowed, dragging her feet as she walked over to him. He was so much taller than she was, when she stood in front of him, they were practically eye level.

"Yes, this is Daddy's play room," he said. "And there will be time to explore. Yes, that's a whipping post, but no, I'm not using it… tonight." Her wide eyes grew even wider. "When we play, we'll try everything out. Little by little. There's time for play and there's time for more serious things. Why are we here *tonight*, Alice?"

"Because I'm… going to get a spanking," she whispered, shifting on her feet. His eyes dropped to her chest and he couldn't help reaching out one hand to grasp a hardened nipple beneath her top. He flicked the pad of his thumb over her nipple, drinking in the sound of her moan. "I… disobeyed you," she said, her eyes closing as he encircled her nipple, his fingers gently grasping her breast. "I… called you names," she whispered. "*Oooohhh.*" His hand had dropped between her legs, up her thigh, past her skirt, and he stroked one finger over her panties, flicking over the soft silk covering her clit. He had to focus. No more of this. He pulled his hand back and anchored both hands on her hips, drawing her so close she stood between his legs, his hardened length pressed up between her thighs.

"That's right," he said. "And did you tell Daddy the truth, little girl?"

She shook her head wordlessly as his hand wrapped around her neck, pulling her closer to him. "You said we need to build trust, Alice. Didn't you, baby?" he whispered in her ear.

She swallowed, her eyes closed tight. "I did. Yes, Daddy."

"There's one thing you're gonna learn, little girl," he said, his fingers massaging the back of her neck. "I always mean what I say. And when you need a spanking, I will always follow through." He paused, taking in her hitched breath, the pad of his thumb tracing her neck, feeling her pulse beat beneath his fingers. "It's time for your spanking, Allie." He pulled back from her and her eyes were half-lidded but guarded, her mouth slightly agape, taking in his massive form and the breadth of his wide lap. He chucked a finger under her chin. "You ever been over a lap, little girl?" he asked softly.

She shook her head wordlessly and he pressed his lips together. She needed stern right now. She needed dependable. She needed her daddy.

"You'll be bare for this."

She began lifting the edge of her blouse, but his large fingers stopped her, palm down.

"No." His hands went to hers and held them. "When Daddy spanks you," he said low, his raspy voice deep and in charge, "and Daddy thinks you need a bare-bottom spanking, Daddy is the one who undresses you."

She swallowed hard as her skirt hit the floor, followed by her panties. He ran his hands over her smooth hips, absolutely gorgeous with her pink mound shaved bare. *Fucking hell*, she was gorgeous. But they had business to take care of. Lifting his hand, he gave her ass one hard, sharp swat. "Over my lap." She froze, her eyes wide, but she didn't move. He frowned, but as he looked at her, he realized she was suddenly afraid. His voice low, he asked her gently, "Do you need Daddy to bring you across his lap?"

She inhaled, seemingly unable to speak, and simply nodded her head. Very well. The point was that she take her punishment, and that he establish trust. If she needed a little help from her daddy to get there, then he was happy to provide it.

"Here, baby," he said, drawing her over to the side of his right knee, then gently pushing her torso over his lap. He was so tall and she so much smaller, her feet came straight off the floor, her blonde hair flying down to cover her face, her hands grasping his leg just above his boots, anchoring herself. Her bare ass over his lap was a sight he wanted to remember forever, hold onto, the smooth silky satin of her naked skin before he painted it red with his handprint. While she'd been ogling his wares, he'd palmed two small implements. But those would wait. He planned on giving her a long, hard spanking she'd remember.

He ran his hand from the top of her thighs, over her ass, to her lower back. She squirmed on his lap.

"You know why Daddy's spanking you, young lady," he said. "We'll start with the name calling. Do you think you spoke to your daddy the right way?" She shook her head wordlessly. Lifting his hand, he brought it down with moderate force. The crack of his hand on her naked skin sounded loudly, and she gasped. A bright pink handprint covered almost her entire ass. *Shit*, that was hot. He administered another swat, then another. "You'll learn to speak respectfully, little girl." *Crack!* "Daddy will speak with respect to his little girl. And my babygirl will treat Daddy with the same respect." *Crack! Crack!* She let out a cry as he built intensity. He could feel the sting in his hand, and no doubt she felt it herself as he upped the swats from moderate force to a bit harder. Now that he'd reddened her whole bottom, she was good and warmed up, and could take more.

"If we're to build trust between us, we'll do it by building respect," he said, punctuating his words with sharp, stinging swats of his hand. He was a master at hand-spanking, his hand slightly curved, then flat, varying the feel of each blow, lifting slowly but descending rapidly. A hard swat landed at the crease of her thighs and ass and she jerked from the pain, but he did not stop. Swat after swat fell, her ass a bright pink now, as he deliberately delivered the spanking he knew she needed. Punishing. Intimate. Every stroke of his hand would drive home his

JANE HENRY & MAISY ARCHER

point. After several dozen good spanks, his palm slowed, smoothing over her flaming hot skin.

"Will you be respectful, Alice?" he asked, his hand poised, ready to spank again.

"Yes!" she gasped. "Yes, Daddy. Yes!"

"Very good," he said. She relaxed.

"Are we done?" she whispered.

He chuckled low. "Oh, honey. I'm just getting started."

Her body tensed as he reached his hand down and picked up the small wooden hairbrush-shaped paddle. It was flat and thick, and he knew the sting would bite deep.

"Let's talk about your safety, now, Allie-girl. Do you think Daddy wants to keep you safe?"

"Yes, Daddy!"

Whack! She screamed out loud as the paddle connected to her pink bottom. He placed one hand around her waist, anchoring her over his lap. The next few swats would be harder for her to take, but she needed them. *Whack!* He delivered another searing swat. "Tonight, you lied about where you were. That put you at risk, little girl. You were with a fucking dipshit I don't trust. One you didn't even know." *Whack!* "That will not happen again. You will tell me where you're going *every.fucking.time.*" *Whack!* She let out a little whimper as the paddle hit the sensitive spot above her thighs. "It will be hard for you, at first. But you'll see it's so I can keep you safe." Another hard swat sounded. "Have I made my point clear about your safety, Alice?"

"Yes," she moaned, her voice shaky now, cracking. She was on the verge of tears. He was getting through. She squirmed and wiggled, trying to get away from the bite of the paddle, but she was no match for him.

"Good," he said, and the small paddle clattered to the floor as he picked up the strap. She moaned, a shiver going through her as he trailed the cool leather along her ass, now bright red. "It's time to finish your spanking. Would it be fair if Daddy let you go now, baby? If Daddy didn't finish your punishment?" She paused, and stilled.

"No, Daddy," she whispered. "I… *lied* to you." The words were barely audible. His instincts had been right. She wasn't where she needed to be. He wanted to let her go now, whip the fucking strap across the room and kiss the pain away. He wanted to hold her close and tell her she'd been brave, and he was proud of her. But this was where he built her trust. If she needed consistent and firm he'd fucking give her what she needed.

The leather strap trailed from the top of her thighs, over her reddened bottom, to the small of her back. She was so perfect, so gorgeous. He was a master musician, and she his instrument. He knew just how to play her, just how to stroke her. His point would be made but she'd be left humming with need. The beauty of a punishment spanking lay not in the intensity but in the method, in the way he spoke to her and brought her over her threshold of pain, just over the edge, emotionally to the state of repentance, so that she well knew he meant what he said. His lecture would remind her that he cared about her. That he wasn't just whipping the hell out of her for his own gratification.

The strap would bring home just how very serious he was, about her safety and obedience. How could he take care of her if she didn't obey?

"You lied, baby," he said. "Daddy will not allow lying. And you disobeyed me. Daddy's gonna strap you soundly for that." He paused. "Am I clear, young lady?"

She tensed as she prepared for the rest of her spanking.

Her voice was shaking, just a whisper, as she responded. "Yes, Daddy."

He lifted the strap, and it whistled through the air before landing hard. She yelped as an angry red stripe rose on her bottom. The strap was serious, but the leather sensual. He could tell, he could feel her stiffen over his lap, braced for the swat. She needed more. "No lying." *Thwap!* A muffled cry. "You'll be fucking honest with your daddy." *Thwap!* A softer cry this time. "I mean what I say, and I want you to remember this." *Thwap! Thwap!* "The next time you even *think* about lying. You think 'Daddy's gonna whip my ass.' " *Thwap!* She did not cry out now, and she did not struggle. He paused, holding the strap in his other hand, he gently ran a hand over her punished backside. "You're taking your punishment like a good girl. Such a very good girl. Daddy's proud of you. But Daddy needs to make sure his little girl *stays* a good little girl." He switched the strap to his right hand, and dished out three more hard, measured swats.

"I'm sorry, Daddy," she choked out.

Was she crying? He heard a loud sniffle.

The strap fell to the floor as he ran one hand slowly over her bottom, hushing her now, soothing.

"That's my good girl, such a good, brave girl," he crooned. This was his favorite part and why he *had* to be a daddy. He couldn't just take what was his. He needed to give back. The sweet give and take made him hard as fucking hell. Her trust, her naked skin soothed under the very hand that had punished her, her soft sniffles as she lay repentant and undone over his knee. "Baby," he said. "You've been holding so much in. Let it out, Allie-girl. My sweet girl." Massaging out the sting was a daddy's prerogative. If he wanted to soothe her, he would. Sure as hell he would. Reaching to the small table beside his chair, he removed a tiny bottle of lotion, and shook some out into his palm. He rubbed his hands together to warm it, then smoothed the warmed lotion over her reddened skin. She sighed, still sniffling, as he gently soothed her.

"Come here, baby," he whispered, lifting her up and into his arms. He bent down and kissed her forehead. His cock strained for release, pushing up against her bottom nestled in his lap, but there would be time for that. Being a patient man meant he would wait for his. She needed him now. She'd just taken one hell of a spanking, and she needed her daddy.

"You all right, baby?" he asked, and she nodded, sniffling.

"Holy shit, you spank hard," she said, but her eyes were bright. She looked as if she would float away right off his lap if he wasn't holding her tight enough.

He fought the smile that threatened to break through, piercing her with a stern look. If he let her off now, thinking that'd been some sort of a game, his efforts would be in vain.

"Damn straight I spank hard," he said in a low growl. "And if you ever fucking do that again, you'll see how hard I can spank. That spanking bench over there isn't for show, little girl. I'll strap you onto that and take Daddy's belt to your ass. You get me?"

Her eyes widened and sobered. "I get you," she whispered.

"Good girl," he said, dipping his head low and taking her mouth. She moaned, her body arching as he kissed her.

He pulled his mouth off and whispered, "Such a good girl," in her ear, while his hands found her breasts once again. His babygirl had been punished. She'd taken her spanking. Now it was time for her reward.

Chapter 5

Alice dumped the pasta into the boiling water, hit the button to start the timer, and gave the pot a half-hearted stir, wishing with all her might that she had time for just a quick nap. She was pretty much BFFs with fatigue, between her jobs, her parents, her volunteer work, and taking care of Charlie, but today she was feeling a special kind of tired. Her emotions were running high, her thoughts were running wild, and she couldn't keep her mind from drifting back to Slay and reliving the night before—the long, hard spanking and the sweet, blissful lovemaking that followed.

Sadly, she knew for a fact that Slay hadn't spent *his* day thinking about *her.* He'd dropped her off to get her car last night, then followed her in his truck to make sure she got home safely and locked her door after Nora left. But today? Only one quick text this morning, reminding her of Daddy's *rules* and letting her know he'd be busy all day, and then dead radio silence.

She hated feeling like a needy, high-maintenance submissive, but *God.* Even Gary the Jerk, with his high-powered finance career, had found time to call or text her at least twice today, not that she'd ever replied to his messages. But Slay, a part-time tattoo artist and club bouncer, couldn't take a quick break to text?

She grabbed a block of cheese from the fridge and began to grate it.

The rhythmic thump of a small foot hitting the kitchen island had her darting a look at Charlie. He'd been perched on a stool there for the past hour, swinging his legs and sketching in his notebook when he should've been doing his daily math work-sheet. His tousled, blonde curls bounced in time with his leg, and above his pink cheeks, still smooth and rounded from babyhood, his deep, serious blue eyes were fixed on his pencil as it scratched lines across the paper. It was on the tip of her tongue to call him out, to remind him angrily that he needed to focus on his *work*, but she held back. *Hypocritical much, Alice?* A litany of all the things *she* hadn't focused on that day swam through her head.

She'd nearly been late getting Charlie to school this morning. She'd messed up orders during the lunch rush at *Cara*. She'd neglected to call and remind the landlord to fix the sink. She'd dropped an entire carton of eggs on the kitchen floor while putting away groceries. And then, putting the cap on her shitty day, she'd completely forgotten (until ten minutes ago) that she had to make two dozen chocolate cupcakes tonight to bring to the Winter Concert fundraising bake sale at Charlie's school tomorrow. The very thought of all that baking, on top of every-thing else, nearly had her in tears, which was completely unlike her. Somehow neither her body nor her brain seemed to be under her control.

Maybe because you obey Daddy *now.*

And just that one stray thought was enough to have her wayward mind spinning back to last night. Her visit to Slay's dungeon-that-wasn't-a-dungeon had been her every fantasy come to life, the spanking so thorough, so erotic, and so perfect that she knew she'd never experience the like again. And call her petty, but she'd be lying if she didn't admit that maybe one of the biggest turn-ons was that she was the first girl he'd ever invited in there. There weren't a lot of firsts left to a guy who'd been around the scene as much as Slay had, and she found that she was incredibly possessive of *this* one.

He'd worked her over so well. *God.* Her ass clenched in memory as she stood in front of the stove, and she could feel the sweet ache again. It was only the second time he'd punished her, yet he'd been able to read her instinctively and know just how far to push to get her to emotional release. She'd been a sub long enough to know how very rare that was.

And that instinctive understanding went even deeper than that. He'd known that she needed to be held and soothed after her punishment. Then he'd known the exact moment when her emotional release gave way to overwhelming arousal.

He'd picked her up, his two enormous hands gently cupping her sore ass and lifting her like she weighed nothing, nudging her to wrap her legs around his waist. He'd stalked out of the play-room he called his office, and then across the living room to the bedroom, his giant tree-trunk legs eating up the distance, all while his busy tongue explored her mouth relentlessly, making her wrap her arms around his neck and hang on for dear life. Then he'd laid her down on his green coverlet, stripped off her blouse and bra, and stood back, drinking in the sight of her, while his eyes burned with raw lust.

She'd tried to reach for him, tried to cover herself, but he'd refused.

"Daddy wants to look at you, baby," he said, his voice clogged with desire. And then he'd reached out one calloused finger to feather gently over her nipple, watching it furl, watching her belly muscles clench. His hot eyes had met hers.

"Christ, you're beautiful, Allie-girl," he'd said, lowering his gorgeous mouth to suck on one stiff peak, and then the other. Then his tongue had moved lower and lower, until she…

"Momma? *Mom!*"

Jesus! Alice whirled away from the counter. "Huh? What?" she demanded.

From his spot at the kitchen island, Charlie giggled. "Momma, the timer has been going off for, like, *eighteen seconds*," he said, his blue eyes dancing with patient humor.

Belatedly, Alice noted the shrill beeping and turned around to shut off the timer. Good Lord, she was a wreck.

She took a deep breath to collect herself, then quickly drained the pasta and set another pot on the stove to start the cheese sauce.

"Sorry, honey," she said. "My mind was a million miles away for a minute there."

"That's what happened to me this morning when I was brushing my teeth. I was imagining I was a superhero, and then I looked out the window and saw the bad guy from the X-men movie."

"Magneto?" Alice asked with a smile as she grabbed butter and milk from the refrigerator.

"*No*! Gosh, Mom! What would *Magneto* be doing out on our street?" he shook his head and Alice shrugged helplessly.

"I meant the senator—you know, the blonde guy with the glasses? Only not as old. Anyway, he was standing in the street outside our house and I knew I had to defeat him with my powers, and it took me a long time to plan the whole thing, and then you were yelling that we were gonna be late." He said the last bit in a reproachful tone that had Alice smothering a chuckle.

She paused to run a hand over his silky blond curls and thought, as she often did, that no matter how many jobs she had to work or cupcakes she had to bake, there was no luckier woman on the planet than she was.

"Mmhmm. Well, next time you see a bad guy out on the street, let me know and we'll defeat him *together*, okay? That way you won't be late."

"*You* can't defeat bad guys," he scoffed. "You don't even like to kill *bugs*!"

"But I do it, Charlie," she said firmly. "Moms do whatever they have to do, even when they don't want to. Including not giving dessert to boys who haven't finished their math by dinnertime." She raised one eyebrow and tapped his half-finished worksheet with her fingertip, before sliding away the paper he'd been covering with pencil sketches of superheroes. "You can work on this more when you're done."

"Okay," he sighed as Alice turned her attention back to the stove.

But a minute later, he piped up, "Hey, Momma? What should I do if I see a big, scary *giant* outside the window?"

Alice shook her head at her boy's imagination. "Oh, definitely call me for giants too. Giants and mutants. Just not spiders," she added under her breath.

"Momma? There's a scary giant outside *right now*."

Alice rolled her eyes. "Wow, you *really* don't wanna do that math homework, huh?"

"No, honest, Momma! Look!"

Alice pursed her lips and turned toward the dark front window, prepared to see a random stack of boxes and trash that might, if she squinted, look like a hulking giant under the glow of the streetlights to an imaginative little boy.

She was absolutely *not* prepared to see Alexander Slater walking up her front steps with a paper grocery bag in one hand and what appeared to be a duffel bag in the other.

Her heart began to pound. Slay was here? *Now*? When she was wearing her rattiest jeans and a t-shirt, with her hair thrown up in a messy knot?

"That's not a giant, sweetie, that's Mr. Slater. Remember? He's my friend from work. He came to your school fair."

"Oh!" Charlie's expression cleared. "Mr. Slater's not scary at all. Not once you know him. I'll go let him in." The boy scrambled off the stool and dashed through the living room, his stocking feet slipping on the hardwood floors.

Alice smoothed her hair and wiped her suddenly-damp palms along her jeans, taking a second to flip the burner off before following with as much calm as she could muster.

"And I thought you were a *giant*!" she heard Charlie confide to Slay, as Slay set down his bags and shucked his coat.

Slay chuckled. "Not the first time I've been called that, bud. You're not far off."

"But you're not a *bad* kind of giant, not like a *frost* giant," Charlie quickly explained, wanting to be sure he hadn't insulted Slay.

Slay's good-natured chuckle turned into a full-on smile, the kind that had nothing to do with humoring his girl's kid and everything to do with truly appreciating Charlie. That smile did dangerous, terrifying things to Alice's heart, and she folded her arms across her chest, as though unconsciously trying to protect herself.

"The frost giants are from the movie *Thor*," Alice hurried to explain, drawing Slay's gaze for the first time. His eyes softened and warmed even further as he looked at her.

"I know who they are, Allie," he interrupted with a wink. Then to Charlie, he added, "Almost too bad I'm not a frost giant, because it's *cold* out there."

"You know who they are? You like *Thor*?" Charlie breathed, wide-eyed. "Do you like X-men, too?"

Slay looked at him like he was crazy. "Of course. Who *doesn't*?"

Charlie looked like he'd won the lottery. "You have to come see my room! I have all the guys *and* all the movies!"

Slay smiled again and ruffled Charlie's hair. "I will, dude. Promise. But first I told your mom I'd take care of some stuff." He leaned down and picked up the bags he'd set on the floor, then turned to look at Alice expectantly.

Alice frowned. "You did?"

Slay raised one eyebrow. "Your kitchen faucet? You said it was spraying water, so I brought my tools. Brought some cookies, too," he said, with a wink and a nod at the grocery bag he carried. "Just in case. Plumbing makes a man hungry."

Alice felt her eyes get wide, and her chest constrict. He'd remembered. She'd mentioned the faucet *once*, during her big tirade the night before and he... he had *remembered*. And then he'd come over, on a cold night in the middle of the week, to fix it.

She felt her eyes start to fill and her nose start to tingle.

"Oh, I'll show you where it is! It was *so* funny, Mr. Slater!" Charlie said, dancing through the living room in front of Slay, leading him to the kitchen. "The other day, Momma turned on the water, and it shot almost all the way up to the cabinet! Like, *pffffft!*" he said, making a sound like an explosion.

Slay chuckled. Then as he walked past her, he took advantage of Charlie's distraction to press a single chaste kiss to her lips and wrap his arm around her waist, steering her towards the kitchen, too.

As she walked alongside him, she thought she couldn't disagree more with Charlie's earlier assessment of the man. The more she got to know Slay, the *scarier* he got—she was in danger of losing her heart to him for good.

Alice gave the kitchen counter a final wipe-down with her rag and sagged against it tiredly. Three dozen cupcakes—enough for the school concert *and* some for Slay to take home with him—

were cooled, frosted, and packed up in the refrigerator, and the kitchen was completely set to rights, including a brand-new gasket on the kitchen faucet that Slay had not only installed, but allowed *Charlie* to *help* install.

She'd invited Slay to dinner after that, of course, and it had gone… well, absolutely perfectly, really. Slay had been sweet and patient with Charlie in the past, taking the boy on rides at Charlie's school fair and getting him dessert when their paths crossed at *Cara*, but Alice had wondered how they'd *really* get along when they were in the same room for an extended period. Slay was so physical—he lifted weights, worked security, was a former soldier. And Charlie was a sensitive kid, an artist, a "nerd," as her father called him.

But she'd forgotten that, as a tattoo artist, Slay knew lots about art and design. Enough to be impressed with Charlie's talent and express that in a way that made Charlie absolutely glow with pride.

And she'd forgotten, too, that Slay was more than just the sum of his parts. The man knew all about Harry Potter, for goodness sake, and proudly discussed it with Charlie. And when Charlie's train of thought had veered abruptly to discussing tanks and guns, Slay had rolled along. He'd seemed completely at-ease with everything the whole night.

Which was more than she could say for herself.

For Alice, the whole evening had been one giant, chest-constricting, heart-stuttering, belly-swooping ride. Despite all the things that she and Slay had done together—the punishments, the sex, even the *daddy* thing—having him in her house, talking to her son, felt like absolutely the most intimate. It broke down a barrier she hadn't consciously understood was there, and now Slay was in every single part of her life.

It was awesome.

It was absolutely freakin' *terrifying*.

She wanted this thing between them to be real and lasting,

God did she ever! And she was willing to work to make it happen. But trusting him as her dom was one thing; trusting him with Charlie felt like another thing completely.

So *what the heck are you gonna do now?*

She knew exactly what Slay would tell her. *Talk to Daddy. Believe Daddy. Do what I tell you.*

She took a deep breath and let it out slowly.

So, okay. That's what she'd do. She'd lay this all out for him. Explain all her fears—about how she needed stability for Charlie, and a father-figure who was a good role model. See what he had to say.

Charlie had gotten into his PJs and brushed his teeth an hour ago. He had towed Slay to his room, eager to show off his drawings and figurines, and to have Slay read him a story. But now it was nearly bedtime, and Alice was ready to have *grownup* time. She filled a cup with water for Charlie, then shut out the light in the kitchen.

She padded down the carpeted hall to Charlie's bedroom, which was situated just down the hall from her slightly larger room. The setup was convenient when Charlie was sick or had a nightmare, and meant there was just enough distance between the rooms to ensure privacy. Not that she was ready to have Slay stay over or anything. It was too soon for that. Still, maybe they could…

"They say I'm stupid."

The bleakness in her baby's voice brought Alice up short, and made her stand, stock-still, in the middle of the hallway, listening to the conversation through Charlie's half-open door.

"Who says that?" Slay asked mildly.

"Kids. At school. I don't do very well with math," Charlie whispered. "Like, at all. I kept having to ask the teacher for help, so now I have to get tutored during recess."

"Huh. They think getting help with math makes you *stupid*?"

Slay sounded confused. "That's crazy. I think that's the smartest thing I've ever heard."

"It is?" Charlie asked, a thread of hope in his voice.

Alice gripped the cup in her hand more tightly. She realized at that moment how deeply Charlie had fallen for Slay and how much he trusted him. Why couldn't it be that easy for her? The man had the power to break not only *her* heart, but her boy's heart as well.

"Bud, everyone's got things that don't come easily, just like everyone has things they're good at and things they're *especially* good at. Some people are really good with words…"

"Like Hillie," Charlie interrupted.

"Yep, like Hillary," Slay agreed. "And some are especially good at cooking, like Tony. And some are really good at keeping other people safe, like Matteo does."

Charlie was silent, but Alice could practically hear the wheels turning in his head.

"Momma's good at lots of things," he finally said. "But what's she 'specially good at?"

Alice pressed her lips together. *Please, God, don't let Slay say anything about taking orders.*

She should have given Slay more credit.

"Your Momma has one of the most special gifts, bud. She makes people happy. She takes care of you, she's a good friend to Hillie and Heidi and Tessa, she helps at your school, she helps me when I need it. And she never asks for anything in return. That's pretty dam—uh, *darn*, special."

Charlie giggled. "That's true."

"So, what kinds of things do these kids say to you? They just teasing, or do they ever get physical?" Slay asked. His voice was casual, but Alice could hear the undercurrent of seriousness that said he was ready to read some parents the riot act if need be. It warmed her heart.

"Nah. Not really. Well, one kid pushed me down on the playground," Charlie admitted. "Once the teacher's aide turned around."

"Did you tell the teacher?" Slay demanded.

"Nah," Charlie repeated. "Grandpa says only *sissies* tattle. He says I should kick the, uh, *crap* out of them, teach them some respect. But, I'm not so good at that."

Alice took a deep breath. She loved her parents dearly, but her father was way too old-school in the how-to-be-a-man department. He was forever telling Charlie "real men" did something or other. She hadn't realized how well Charlie had listened.

Seemed there were a lot of things she hadn't realized.

"Hey! Slay, you know how to hit, right? You could show me!" Charlie continued excitedly. "You could teach me how to fight back!"

Oh, no way. Alice took an instinctive step towards the room, ready to intervene. But once again, Slay was more than capable of handling the situation.

"How about I teach you something better than that?" Slay suggested.

"Like what?"

"Charlie, violence should always be a last resort, you know?" Slay's voice was deep and patient.

"I… guess?" Open skepticism from the six-year-old. She couldn't wait to hear how Slay would handle this. She heard him blow out a breath and regroup.

"Okay, let's look at it like this. You're a special kid and have special talents, right? You're like… an X-man. You're one of the good guys."

Alice clasped a hand over her mouth to hold back the bubble of helpless laughter that threatened to spill over. Charlie was an X-man? *Oh, Slay.*

"And those kids who tease you? They're like the humans who want to get rid of the X-men, yeah? Totally in the wrong, no question. Bad guys. But if you hit back without thinking, if you

78

fight them when you could have found a more peaceful solution…"

"I become a villain, too. Like Magneto!" Charlie's voice was a horrified whisper.

"Exactly," Slay agreed grimly. "Not worth it."

"So, you're saying I should never hit back?"

"No, Charlie. If someone's trying to hurt you or someone you love, you need to protect yourself. I'm just saying to look for other options first. Fighting's the last resort," Slay repeated. "Not the first."

Charlie sighed. "I get it. If they push me again, I'll tell someone."

"Good," Slay approved. "Bud, when someone says something that hurts you, no matter who it is, you need to really listen to what they're saying and use your own judgment to decide if it's the truth or a lie. If it's true, you own your mistake and correct it. But if it's a lie, like those kids saying you're stupid, you ignore it. Flat out. Good men don't waste their time or energy convincing liars that they lie. You focus on the people who really know you, the people who have faith in you and love you, and you let that other shi—uh, *stuff*, go. You get me?" He paused, and Alice could just imagine Charlie nodding seriously on the other side of the door. She pressed her toes into the carpet and squeezed her eyes shut, her chest tight with emotion.

Charlie was silent for a moment, digesting all this, then he asked, "Slay, were kids ever mean to you when you were a kid?"

"Nah. I was big, and kids were scared of me even back then," Slay said. Then he added softly, "But my dad made up for it."

Alice's heart broke at the implications of those words, and she remembered the one sour note at dinner. After Slay had scarfed down a mammoth portion of her homemade mac and cheese, declaring it the absolute best he'd ever eaten with such sincerity that she couldn't help but believe him, she'd teasingly asked, "Didn't your mom make mac and cheese?" He'd said only, "Not that I recall," and then changed the subject abruptly.

Now, he explained to her son in that same deep, patient voice, "My mom wasn't around when I was a kid, it was just my sister, my dad, and me. And my dad… Well, he was a lot like your Grandpa sounds. He loved me, so he wanted me to be strong. He didn't tolerate any weakness."

Charlie made a considering noise. "Was he hard on your sister, too?"

Slay snorted. "No. Elena had him wrapped around her finger from day one. Had *me* wrapped around her finger, too. Little sisters are like that."

"I wish I had a sister," Charlie said.

"I'll share mine with you," Slay offered. "I warn you, she's a nurse and she teaches yoga in her free time. She might twist you up into a pretzel and then warn you not to eat too much sugar. But she's *really* good at math."

Charlie giggled. "I think I'll like her!"

Oh, Lord. One more person for Charlie to get attached to?

Alice didn't wait to hear how Slay responded. She sucked in a deep breath, plastered on a wide smile, and stepped into Charlie's room. "Bedtime!" she called.

Charlie, all cozied up in his footie pajamas, was sitting cross-legged at one end of his red-and-blue-striped bed with a mass of multicolored action figures splayed out around him. Slay sat on the floor, propped up against the side of the bed, a story book face-down on his lap and his arms folded over his chest, watching Charlie intently.

God, he *did* look like a giant, sprawled across the floor of her little boy's room, with a swath of light from Charlie's race car lamp spilling across his broad shoulders and long, long legs. He should have seemed out of place in the room, crowded and uncomfortable.

He didn't. Instead, he made the whole room seem somehow warmer and cozier and… safer.

"It's a school night, honey," Alice told Charlie. "Gotta get to sleep."

"But wait, Momma," Charlie argued. "I needed to ask Slay a question."

"Slay?" she asked, raising one eyebrow significantly. "You mean *Mr. Slater*?"

Charlie shook his head. "He said I could call him Slay!" he said excitedly. "He said all his friends do! And he gave me his business card with his phone number on it and told me I could call him whenever I needed to!"

Alice looked at Slay, who shrugged.

"Okay," Alice agreed. "But you can ask Slay your question later, okay? Another day."

"But it'll be too late later!" Charlie cried. "I wanted to ask him to come to the Winter Concert at school!"

Alice felt her eyes widen.

Slay? At the Winter Concert. At the ultra-conservative Pevrell and Brahms School?

"Isn't that okay?" Charlie's face screwed up in a frown, and Alice quickly masked her expression.

"Sure. Sure, if he wants to." She turned to Slay, but couldn't meet his eyes. "It's a week from tomorrow, the Wednesday before Christmas," she explained. "It's, um, formal. Parents have to wear suits and dresses. And you might already have plans, or have to work, or…"

"I'll be there," Slay said.

"You will?" Charlie repeated excitedly, his blue eyes shining.

"You will?" Alice asked, more dubiously.

"Definitely," Slay confirmed.

With the grace that always seemed to startle her, Slay levered to his feet without using his hands. He closed the storybook and set it gently on Charlie's nightstand.

"Charlie, man, it's been a pleasure," Slay said, standing next to the bed. He extended his hand to Charlie, who clasped it in some unusual guy grip that seemed to satisfy both of them.

"Same here, Slay," Charlie said seriously, sounding so grown-up and manly despite his high-pitched baby voice that her lips twitched and her heart ached.

Slay nodded once. "Night, bud."

Then he turned to her and said, "I'll meet you in the hall."

When he had gone, Alice set Charlie's water on his night-stand and helped him crawl under the covers, sweeping all of his action figures back into their plastic tub.

Charlie let out an enormous yawn. "Maybe when it's spring-time, Slay can help me ride my bike. I bet he knows how to ride a bike, don't you think? Maybe we should ask him."

In the *spring*. It was way too soon to be thinking about what Slay would be doing with them in the spring… wasn't it?

Alice shook her head and stroked a hand through his blond curls. "Maybe you should roll over and close your eyes, and we'll worry about that later, okay?"

"Okay, Momma," Charlie agreed sleepily, already rolling over and making himself comfortable.

She kissed his soft cheek, turned off the big light, and backed out, shutting the door.

She paused with her hand still on the knob and took a breath. She had to go talk to Slay about all the things that had been worrying her, but what in the world would she say? How in the world would she *begin?*

"He's a great kid."

Slay's deep voice, pitched low, came from the far end of the hallway, and she instinctively turned toward him.

"He is," she agreed, walking over to stand in front of him.

"What happened with his dad? Why isn't he around?" There was a definite thread of anger in his voice, anger on Charlie's behalf.

Alice took a minute to let the sweetness of that slide through her before she replied.

"Last I heard, he was living in Concord with his wife."

"Concord is thirty minutes from here. In traffic," Slay said.

"Yup. And it might as well be a million miles away," she said. She slid past him and down the hall, flipping the kitchen light back on as she went. She was going to need tea, if not something stronger, to get through this conversation.

Though the man made not a single sound, she could feel him behind her, angry and comforting all at once, and knew he'd followed.

"His dad's name is Derek," Alice began, as she grabbed the kettle from the stove and filled it with water. "We were in high school sweethearts. You know the drill—I was the perky cheerleader, he was the student council president. His mom is rich, my parents are solidly middle-class, but we didn't care. We were going to be President and First Lady someday and it would make a great story." She rolled her eyes at her own innocence and set the water over the flame.

"We had sex once, Slay. *One time*. It wasn't planned. We were saving ourselves for marriage, you know? But things got out of hand and it happened. One. Time. Without protection."

She turned to look at him then, suddenly desperate to see how he was taking all of this. He had stopped in the doorway from the hall and was leaning one shoulder against the wall. His face was blank and set, his arms folded over his chest, and she was somehow thrown back to the night she'd had to tell her parents that her *one time* had resulted in a pregnancy. The shame of it had been crippling.

But damn it, she was way beyond that now. Screw anyone who wanted to judge her based on her past. She stood up straighter.

"That was that," she continued. "When I told Derek I wanted to keep the baby, he told me I was crazy. Told me he had as much say in the matter as I did, and he didn't want a kid."

Slay made a growling noise that Alice couldn't interpret.

"To be fair," she allowed, "Derek said he was thinking of me, too. I had a bright future ahead of me. I had a scholarship to BU. We had this whole *plan*. Kids were supposed to come later, after grad school. And as far as he was concerned, I was the one throwing a wrench in the works, throwing everything away. So, needless to say, he's not involved in Charlie's life."

"He should pay…" Slay began, but Alice cut him off with a shake of her head.

"No. Charlie's *mine*. I mean, maybe if I went to court, he'd end up paying me child support, but then what if he decides, a few years down the line, that he actually wants to get involved in Charlie's life and play at being his dad? Not gonna happen. Not if I can help it. It sucks financially right now, but it keeps my boy protected." She looked at Slay seriously and continued, "That's the most important thing, Slay. Protecting Charlie."

He got what she was saying. He unfolded himself from the wall and strode forward until their chests were nearly touching. "I swear to you, Alice, that I will never do anything to hurt you or Charlie. I told you before, and now I'm going to say it again: I'm all-in with this. With you. With him."

He lifted one hand and brushed a strand of hair back from her forehead. *So sweet.* She felt herself melting.

"Why didn't you call me today?" she blurted out, startling both of them.

"What?" Slay blinked.

"You didn't call or text. Yeah, you said you'd be busy. But too busy to take a break or check in? Because what if something happened to me or to Charlie, Slay? You can't… you can't just *take day off.* You can't just decide to only be available when it's convenient."

The words poured out of her, every needy, whiny, helpless

thought she tortured herself with. She was mortified, but she couldn't stop.

"And I don't blame you, really I don't. It's a lot to take on— I've got a kid, I've got this busy, complicated life, clearly I sound like a *crazy person* half the time," she said with a laugh that sounded more like a sob. "But I just…"

"Allie," he said. One word, and it stopped her tirade like a cork in a bottle.

His arms came around her and one hand came up to grip her jaw firmly, forcing her to look at him.

"Babe, I explained to you this morning that I had a busy day. And *yeah*, it *was* too busy to take a break or check in." His voice was rough and direct. "I don't just work at *Inked* or at The Club, babe. I have private security work I do, too, with some former Marine buddies of mine." He glanced significantly at his arm, where his shirt covered the bullet-hole scar he'd acquired when he and some of the security guys he worked with had helped to rescue Nora.

Alice took a shuddering breath. She *did* know that he had friends who did that. She hadn't realized how involved he was. "I'm being crazy, aren't I?"

"You're being cautious," he corrected. "I get it. And *because* I get it, because I get that you need to protect Charlie, too, I'm working as hard as I can to be patient with you about this. But babe, you *need* to trust me if this shit's going to work. It's not easy, maybe it's not instinctive, I know. But you've gotta trust me enough to come to me, to share this shit with me, so that we can talk through it, so it doesn't build up and drive you insane. You've gotta trust that I'm not going to roll over you and abandon you when you do. I'm not that dickhead. You get me?"

God, is that what she had been doing? Comparing Slay to Derek? Not believing that Slay would stick around because Derek hadn't? Judging *Slay* based on *his* past, even though she loathed it when people did that to her? Slay hadn't done *one single thing* to suggest that she couldn't trust him. She was being silly and, worse, unfair. And she was fighting against the most amazing thing to happened to her since Charlie was born, the one thing she wanted most.

"I get you, Daddy," she said.

It was the first time she'd said it without prompting, fully clothed and not crazed with lust. It was the first time she'd voluntarily acknowledged exactly what was growing between them, and she knew he recognized it when his beautiful brown eyes softened… then heated.

The hand gripping her jaw slid back to grab the hair at the back of her head, pulling her head back as his lips descended on hers. His kiss was hard and wet, bruising and claiming. She wrapped one hand around his broad shoulder and the other around the smooth column of his neck, and held on for dear life.

A minute later, he eased back and set his lips on her forehead.

"Here's what we're going to do," he said, reluctance clear on his face as he stepped back and grabbed her hand, reaching out to turn off the flame under the kettle as though he knew the last thing she needed was more caffeine. "Tonight, we're going to watch TV. There's this spy show my buddy keeps telling me I have to see, and we'll check it out together."

"We will?" she asked in confusion. At that moment, if he'd made a move to lead her down the hall and spank her in her bedroom, she likely wouldn't even have protested, she was so consumed by the kiss.

"Correct me if I'm wrong, but you probably don't want me sleeping over, yeah?"

"God, no. I mean, *yes*. Yes, I don't think that's a good idea. Not yet. Not… with Charlie," she stammered.

He chuckled. "Right. So, TV?"

She nodded.

"And then," he continued. "You're working tomorrow, right?"

So then you'll see if you can get Nora to watch Charlie on Thursday, and you and I will go on a date."

"A *date?* Like we'll go back to your apartment and you can show me your playroom again, that kind of date?" she asked eagerly.

He raised one eyebrow. "A date, like, I'll pick you up and you'll go along with whatever happens. Yeah?"

This trusting business got easier and easier.

"Yeah, Daddy," she agreed, and let him tow her to the couch.

Chapter 6

"Is Charlie a light sleeper?" Slay asked, trying to sound serious.

"God, Slay! No, he's a heavy sleeper but *not heavy enough.*" Alice pulled back off his lap and furrowed her brow at him, her blue eyes serious and golden hair framing her face so that it looked like a sort of halo.

He gave himself away with a low chuckle. She was fun to tease.

Balling her fist up with a grin, she smacked him in the belly, but he grabbed her wrist and sobered. "I was teasing you," he said. "But it's not okay to hit me, not even when you're playing." He paused for a few seconds, letting his words sink in. "You understand?"

She looked suitably embarrassed, and nodded, casting her eyes down. He smiled at her, stroking her hair with pride. His little Allie-girl was learning. There was no need to remind her of the consequences of disobedience every time he gave her an instruction. She knew now that he meant what he said, and that disobeying him would earn her a spanking. They were making progress.

But it wasn't all about teaching her to obey, and meting out necessary discipline. There were other things that had to happen in their relationship, things he'd neglected. That was why he was here. He remembered the way she'd looked the night before when he'd crashed her date and hauled her ass out of there. The way her eyes had flashed at him and she'd insisted he earn his keep.

I'm not some random, stereotypical babygirl.

He'd been watching her for months, testing her, waiting until the time was right, but like a total asshole, hadn't taken into account *what she needed.* She needed so much more than discipline and structure, hot sex against the wall of The Club and a man to call Daddy. Alice Cavanaugh was fearless and brave. In the years he'd spent at The Club, he'd never met a submissive who would stand up to him, look him in the eye the way she did, and tell a man twice her size with the potential to spank the hell out of her to get his shit together and *make him earn her trust.*

It was only one of so many reasons *why* he wanted Alice to be his.

"Come here, baby," he said, drawing her into his lap. "It's time we talked about a few things." He pulled her closer to him, and God she looked amazing in her dark-colored jeans, thread-bare light blue t-shirt that accentuated her curves, and messy bundle of hair. Closing his eyes briefly, he let himself feel the longing for her that he'd been fighting for so long.

As she nestled into his lap, her head on his chest, he took in her surroundings with the eye of a man trained to notice details. The living room was tidy, but the couch had seen better days. Still, it was warm and welcoming. A popsicle-stick structure painted in garish red and yellow stripes stood on the end table. Slay could easily imagine her gushing praise to Charlie when he showed her his craft with pride. A pile of children's books sat next to a few well-worn paperbacks. The television was small, mounted above a small black entertainment center, and a few framed pictures stood on the shelves of the unit. Alice, looking as gorgeous as ever but younger, holding a chubby blond baby. Charlie as a little toddler, holding out his hands. Another picture of Charlie being held between a couple that looked a bit like Alice but more reserved. Her parents?

Looking down at Alice, Slay realized her eyes were closed. Was she asleep?

"You awake, honey?"

"Mmm," she said. "It just feels *so nice* being held by you like this."

His arms instinctively tightened around her. "Take what you need, Allie," he said, and without giving it much thought, he whispered what he felt out loud. "You're safe here, babygirl." It was what he loved best about being a daddy. Being a large, strong man meant he could offer the sort of protection his babygirl needed, and her depending on him fulfilled his own strong desire to protect. It was in his blood.

"Who knew," Alice whispered, a small smile playing at her lips. "Who knew such a big, strong guy like you could be so sweet?"

"Sweet?" he said with a chuckle. "I wouldn't say I'm sweet."

"Of course you wouldn't. That's what's so sweet about it."

"That's crazy talk, girl."

She smiled knowingly. "Suit yourself, big guy."

Reaching down, he gave her a sharp swat, making her squirm on his lap.

"Charlie's down the hall," she protested.

"We'll have to find a way around that, honey," he said. "I'll be discreet. We'll come up with some code words, and I've got some very quiet tools in my arsenal. But I'm not gonna stop being your daddy because there are people around."

She lifted her head from his chest, frowning. "You can't spank me with Charlie in the house! He'll hear you!"

Can't?

Reaching a hand to the nape of her neck, he grasped her golden tresses and pulled sharply, her head tugging back and her eyes widening. He lowered his mouth to her ear. "You behave yourself, Allie-girl," he said sternly. Another tug of her hair. "Like I said, I can be discreet. I'll respect your space. But you *will* obey me, and if you don't, you'll be punished. If I have to wait, I'll wait. We'll talk it through and find ways to make this ours without losing our privacy. But no matter what, you answer to me. You get me?"

He saw the struggle in her eyes. She wanted to push back, and yet she wanted to submit. In the end, she chose to submit. "Yes, Daddy."

His cock hardened, adrenaline surging through him. *Yes, Daddy.* Shit.

Releasing her hair, he nodded. "Good girl. So let's talk. First, yes, you don't want me to be overheard by Charlie. Of course I get that. We'll find ways to be quiet. Yeah?"

She nodded.

"We've already talked about your rules, and you're learning. I'm proud of you." Her eyes warmed and she looked at him shyly. "There will be times you disobey me. I'll spank you, and we'll talk it out, but we'll move on. Got it?"

She squirmed on his lap. "Yes, Daddy."

He smiled at her. "At The Club? There's no being discreet. Every fucking dominant there will know you are mine. No more dabbling in scenes. You're by my side and you'll do what I say. You get me?"

Though her eyes widened, she nodded.

"Good girl. But there's more to this than spanking your ass." He ran his large, rough fingers through her golden hair, trailing from the top of her scalp to the nape of her neck. "A daddy likes to take care of his little one. It's a daddy's prerogative. You all right with that?"

Her eyes closed and she sighed. "Who wouldn't be okay with that?" she asked.

"Lots of people, baby," he said, as he pulled her back onto his chest.

"Well, not this girl," she said.

"Good. Then this is what I want you to do. When you need me, you tell me. Yeah?"

She nodded. "Yeah," she said. "I could do that."

He nodded. They'd see about that. "And you give me space to take care of you." He paused. "Can you handle that?"

She snorted. "Of course I can!"

He smiled to himself. It might not always be as easy as she thought. Bit by bit, he'd show her. Now was as good a time as any. "It's getting late, Alice. I want you to go get ready for bed, and then come back to me."

Alice sat up, frowning. "Seriously? It's like two hours before I go to bed."

Leaning toward her, he took her chin in hand. "Did I say you have to go to bed right now?"

Understanding dawned as she shook her head. "No," she whispered.

"But if you don't do what Daddy says, you *will* go to bed, and I do mean now. Is that clear?"

Her mouth dropped open. "Oh. Well. Okay, yes. Yes, Daddy," she said, getting to her feet and scurrying down the hallway as he delivered a helpful swat to her ass. Shit, he hoped she had some PJs with good coverage. If she returned wearing something skimpy, he was a goner.

She came back in a tiny pair of plaid boxer shorts that barely covered the curves of her ass cheeks and a teeny tiny white cami with her nipples poking straight through. She was all creamy curves and contours.

Shit.

Her eyes widened at the look on his face. "What?" she said.

"You told me to get ready for bed, so I did." She'd pulled out her ponytail holder and her hair tumbled about her shoulders. He blinked. What had she said again?

She was frowning. "I thought I did what you told me to," she began, but by now she was in reaching distance so he snagged her around the waist and pulled her straight onto his lap.

"These are your jammies?" he half-growled.

Alice giggled on his lap. "You call them jammies?"

"Just did," he said. "And yeah, baby, you did what Daddy said. What you didn't do was make it any fucking easier for me to keep my hands and my mouth off you."

"Ohhh," she said, comprehension dawning as her eyes twinkled. Her voice dropped, low and sultry. "No self control?"

He growled, pulling her closer to him. "Careful, little girl. Daddy might have to punish you for being naughty."

"Oh yeah?" she said in a breathless whisper. "How would Daddy punish me?"

"Stand you in the corner," he whispered. "Send you to bed early. Lots of ways to make you behave, honey." He tucked a stray lock of her hair back. Although they were both smiling, and the mood was playful and sexy, he meant every word. He *would* stand her in the corner or send her to bed if she misbehaved.

She leaned in closer. "Would you *spank* me, Daddy?" she whispered.

He moaned, grabbing her ass and squeezing firmly. "Course I would. You damn well know it."

She closed her eyes and sighed.

He stroked her hair as he spoke to her. "A few ground rules, Allie-girl. We've got most of those in place. You know I expect you to behave. But I also want to make sure you take care of yourself. I'll make sure you eat your meals, and get to bed on time. Got it, baby? Tonight, I want you in bed in an hour. That's reasonable. And you make sure you eat breakfast before you take off for work tomorrow. Got it?"

She nodded.

"Good girl. Now come and rest your head on me while we watch a show. Okay, baby?"

She nodded again, curled herself up on his lap and rested her head on his chest while he picked out a home improvement traveling show, not something he normally watched, but she said she loved it. But before the globe-trotting couple had picked out the charming villa on the Mediterranean, Alice was fast asleep on his chest. He stroked his hand through her hair. She looked so much younger when she was asleep, without the cares of the world on her shoulders. God, he wanted to give that peace to her *every* day. He held her like that for a while, holding her against his chest, arms tucked around her. But finally, it was time to get her to bed.

It was an easy matter to get to his feet and take her in his arms. Her head fell against his shoulder. Dipping his head down, he kissed her forehead as he stalked to her bedroom. He peeked in at her rooms as he walked. She had what looked like an office or guest room across from Charlie's, but hers was a good distance away down the hall. He was pleased to see the arrangement. A bedroom straight across from Charlie's could get… interesting.

When he reached her room, it was dark, but he could just make out the shadow of her dresser and bed. Crossing the room in a few large strides, he placed her down on the bed. She woke as he laid her down.

"Oh, I must've fallen asleep," she murmured.

"Sleep now, baby," he whispered. "Do you have a spare key? I'll lock the door behind me."

"In the drawer next to my bed," she said, her eyes shut.

His phone buzzed obnoxiously in his pocket.

Damn. A text that couldn't wait.

They're on the move. Go. Meet me at central ASAP.

He opened the drawer and removed the keys. Alice stirred.

"I need to go now, baby," he said. "Work call. You be a good girl, get some sleep and text me in the morning. Yeah?"

She nodded sleepily. "Yes. Night, Daddy."

He leaned in and kissed her cheek, tucking the blanket up around her shoulders and around her back. "Sleep well, baby."

It took all his willpower to walk out the door.

Diego Santiago sat in the cramped office, a little hole-in-the-wall room that was off the grid, a single lamp burning on a bare desk so small Slay had to move his legs to the side because he couldn't fit them underneath. Diego's jaw clenched, arms crossed so tightly his muscles bulged and flexed, his long, sturdy legs out in front of him with his ankles crossed. His firm jaw sported a five-o'clock shadow, and his longish black hair fell over his forehead. His coffee-colored eyes were mere slits of fury, and full lips pursed. Slay leaned against his desk, nodding.

"Let's go over every detail," he said. "One at a time. Salazar sent a man over to Westland Community College, fed off some students there and passed out some smack, but took two girls who wanted to barter rather than pay."

Diego's nostrils flared. "Yup."

Slay ran a hand over his shaved head. "Question, Diego. Any of those girls happen to be tight with Nora?"

Diego's jaw clenched even tighter. "Yep. One of them goes to Nora's high school and is taking the same dual enrollment class at WCC that Nora's in. *Fucking* hell, Slay. It's so goddamn hard to keep my mouth shut and stay tight with these sons of bitches."

Slay nodded once. "When do you think you'll have enough to bring this whole circus down? Haul their asses to jail?"

"End of the month."

Slay's brows shot up. A one-year undercover gig of epic proportions was about to go down, and he'd be part of putting their asses behind bars. Quickly, his thoughts went to Alice. The closer they came to the end of the investigation, the more dangerous it would be for all of them. He couldn't share details with her, of course. She'd better do what she was goddamned told so he could keep her safe.

"You've got shit on Salazar's screwing underage girls in the past. These two he took this weekend… they were over eighteen, so not underage. Consensual?"

Diego gave one curt nod. Shit. They couldn't slap that on his ass then. Still, there were ways to make him pay.

"So you're pissed over this one because you're closin' in, and the mother fucker decides to rain on your girl's stomping grounds."

Diego's eyes shot away from Slay's. He snorted. "Nora is hardly *my* girl."

"Cut the shit, Santiago. You've been all over her since we got her out of Salazar's clutches a couple months ago. Nothing wrong with that. Nothing to hide. No shame, brother."

Diego met his eyes. "Nothing to hide, except the fact that I'm undercover in Chalo's organization. The chick thinks I'm a fucking drug dealer and pimp. She looks at me like I'm lower than scum."

Slay continued. "But you know you can't let personal feelings get in the way of making the right call."

Diego frowned and his jaw clenched. "Yeah. I know it."

"So tell me what you know about Salazar's connections to Pevrell and Brahms."

"Jesus, those filthy rich parents over there are no better than—"

"Watch it. My girl's kid goes there."

Diego paused, meeting Slay's eyes squarely, though Slay dwarfed him in both size and age. "You can't let personal feelings—"

"Shut it, Santiago."

Diego's eyes danced, but he nodded. "Seems there's a woman whose kid goes to P&B who got herself hooked on Chalo's product. Gary Levitz was her contact. He let her run up a tab, and she can't make the payments. High as fuck, those payments. So a few months ago, seems Levitz made her a proposition. She's trafficking Chalo's "clean" shit, high end, pricey. Got a safe tucked away in her townhouse in town, and a few "clients." But now Chalo is turning up the heat. Gary's been getting sloppy with his contacts. Nailin' the chick on the side, cutting her some slack."

Levitz, the same asshole who'd been eating pasta with Alice. Slay's hands fisted as Diego continued.

"Gary has to make a play, get back in Chalo's good graces. He's got what Salazar is calling his Santa special coming in this weekend. The college kids leave for Christmas break soon, and he's ready to make a move. Get them more invested. Finals are over their heads, gotta go home to their moms and dads and give a good report. So he's getting a couple more students to push at the college, and having the woman at P&B push her stuff heavily so she can get her kid shit for Christmas." He paused and took a deep breath. "And Levitz has been eyeing your girl. Last night, the woman from P&B called Alice."

"Because there's a fucking bake sale," Slay said.

Diego shrugged. "Could be. Keep an eye on it, brother. It was the same woman Levitz and Salazar are in *tight* with, Mindy Freeman. I wouldn't want any girl of mine to have any ties to Levitz or anyone else who works for Chalo."

Slay's heart was beating in a tempo he could hardly control, the blood pounding in his ears. If he ever got those bastards in a room alone…

But no. He had to keep his shit together. In the morning, Alice would call him and he would make plans to take her on a real date. He'd wine and dine her, and if the timing was right, take her back to his room. He needed to build trust, and it would happen in more ways than one.

He pushed himself to standing. "Thanks for the update, Santiago. Things will move over the next week."

Diego unfolded himself from his chair, and they shook hands briefly, Diego's grip so tight it would make a lesser man wince, but Slay liked the firm grip. They both knew without having to say it that in the next week, anything could happen. They'd both been on the rescue side of an operation, and both had seen brothers taken down in the line of duty. It was crucial he and Diego had each other's backs. If all went as planned, Salazar's ring could be annihilated. Alice and Nora and all the other innocents in this would be spared the shitty details, and be safe once again.

As they walked to the exit, Diego turned to Slay. "Man on Alice tonight says all looks quiet. But watch your back, brother."

Slay wanted to be there. He wanted to be under her roof. But if she were going to trust him, he couldn't push himself on her. He had to prove himself trustworthy.

He nodded as he opened the door to the hallway. "Keep her safe, Santiago."

Chapter 7

Alice tugged experimentally on the hem of the red dress and eyed the reflection in her full-length mirror critically. The dress was simple and lovely, with long sleeves that stretched just past her wrists and a neckline high enough that even her mother might find it conservative. But it was shorter than she was used to. Way, *way* shorter. And the word *tight* did not begin to describe the indecent way the stretchy fabric caressed her body.

In the mirror, she saw three sets of eyes watching her, and three feminine heads nodding in approval, but she wasn't convinced. "I just don't know," she said dubiously, twisting back and forth. "It's not really... *me?*"

Three exclamations of disbelief greeted this statement and made Alice smile.

This experience of having a group of girlfriends in her bedroom helping her prepare for a date was a completely new experience for her. Being a really young mom had made close friendships challenging—most of the other moms in Charlie's class were a good deal older than Alice, and most of the women Alice's age were just beginning to think about settling down and having kids. But somehow, in just the past few months, Alice had found a group of women who accepted her (*and* Charlie) with open arms, almost like… family.

From the spot she'd co-opted at the foot of Alice's bed, Tessa Damon—the manager of *Cara*, who had become Alice's boss a few months ago and her trusted friend soon after that—shook her long auburn hair back and made a noise of disagreement. "Honey, it's so *totally* you. Put the shoes on and you'll see," she said, nodding toward the strappy black heels on the floor. "It fits you like a glove. And you have the perfect figure for it—not too small and not too *big*, unlike some of us." She looked from Alice's moderate curves, then down at her own impressive bust line, and sighed. "Heidi let me borrow it for a party Tony and I went to a couple weeks ago, and I didn't get past my own front door."

Alice met Tess's eyes in the mirror and frowned. "You mean because the dress was uncomfortable?"

Heidi, the second member of the trio, who was sprawled on the bed next to Tess, shook with laughter in a way that made her long, brown ponytail dance. Her pretty blue eyes flashed as she prompted knowingly, "Yeah, explain what you *mean*, Tess!"

Tess shot Heidi a glare, though her eyes were lit with humor. "No, the dress was perfectly *comfortable*," she explained to Alice. "But Tony took one look at me and went all caveman! 'Oh, *hell*, no!' " she said, in a decent parody of Tony's deep voice. " 'No way. *My woman* is not going out in public in that thing.' Practically started beating his chest. I'm guessing you ladies know the drill." She rolled her eyes, but her soft smile said she loved her guy's possessive, protective nature.

It was hard for Alice to imagine Tony Angelico, the most laid-back boss in the history of bosses, as the alpha-dominant type, but when it came to his woman, Tony had no problem letting his inner caveman loose.

Heidi shook her head fondly. "Those Angelico brothers. They're so cute when they regress." Alice figured Heidi would know, considering she was married to the oldest of the three Angelico brothers, Dominic.

Heidi's younger sister, Hillary, who had been sitting on the slipper chair in the corner scrolling through something on her phone, with her short, wavy reddish-brown hair pulled back in a thin, silver headband, glanced up at this. "I dare you to tell Dom he's cute when he regresses, Heids. Heck, I dare you to tell *Matt* that," she snickered, referring to her boyfriend, Matteo, who happened to be Dom's twin brother and Slay's best friend.

Heidi shot Hillie a withering glance. "No way, Tinker Bell!" she teased, using the nickname that made the petite, formerly-blonde Hillary scowl. "You can taunt your man yourself. I don't need any help getting in trouble."

Heidi turned back to Tess with a wide, innocent smile. "Now, if our mom were here, she'd tell you that was the perfect opportunity to educate Tony on how, as a mature, independent woman, you won't allow a man to dictate what clothing you put on your body. Maybe throw in some things about how you're not responsible for men's reactions to you, and how you own your sexuality."

Tess pursed her lips and nodded solemnly. "Yup. I really *should* have educated him. But you know, Tony and I got a little *distracted* after that. Missed opportunity, I guess." She and Heidi exchanged a glance, and both burst out laughing.

Alice shook her head in amusement at the back-and-forth as she wriggled her feet into the shoes.

"I wore that dress exactly once," Heidi said. Her blue eyes twinkled and the diamonds in her wedding ring flashed in the lamplight as she sat up. "Back in October, Dom and I went to dinner with Paul and John at this lovely little inn out in Concord. It was a little bit chilly, so I wore a shawl over the dress, but when we got to the restaurant, I took the shawl off." She snickered at the memory. "Oh, there was chest-beating aplenty. Dom glared at anyone who looked at me, even the poor waiter. John told me after the fact that he thought Dom was ready to pee in a circle around me."

The women, including Alice, all laughed. John was the pastry chef at Tony's restaurant, *Cara*, so Alice knew him fairly well. And she knew that although he *looked* like a blue-eyed angel, he had the most snarky and hilarious sense of humor… especially when his boyfriend and dominant, Paul, wasn't there to keep him in check. She could totally picture him saying this.

"And, you know, strangely enough, when we got home, *we* got all *distracted*, too," Heidi mused with a grin. "I think it must be something with that dress that guys just can't resist!"

Hillary and Tess exchanged a glance, and Tess pressed her lips together to suppress a laugh.

Hillary didn't bother. "Yeah, it was totally just the *dress* that Dom found distracting, Heids," she deadpanned. "Otherwise, you two would've been watching Law and Order reruns all night like you usually do, right?"

In reply, Heidi grabbed a small pillow off the bed and lobbed it at her smiling sister, who batted it away without looking up from her phone.

"I think you'll need to borrow the dress next, Hillie. You must need a little *distraction* in your life if you're sitting over there on your phone while we're talking about our guys!" Tess teased. "Are you playing that candy game?"

Hillary sighed and put her phone down. "No! I'm just trying to figure out my, um, calendar. Something's off, I think." She shook her head and waved a hand through the air dismissively. "Whatever. Anyway, I doubt I would get the same results with that dress. I'm so short that it would come down past my knees and I don't have Tessa's *assets* to fill out the front of it. I'd look like a pilgrim."

"Aw. And you and Matteo aren't into naughty-pilgrim role play?" Tess teased.

Hillie snorted and grabbed the pillow back up off the floor to launch it at Tessa. "I think we'll leave the pilgrim roleplay to you and Tony."

Tess giggled and caught the pillow. "It could be fun!" she protested.

"Hush, both of you!" Heidi laughed. "Charlie will be home soon!"

At Heidi's words, Alice caught sight of the clock and had a mini panic attack. "Ladies, I love you, but you're not helping me!" she groaned. "I'm freaking out just a little bit over here. I have no idea what Slay's plans are for tonight, I'm not sure how to dress for this date, this guy I went on *one* date with keeps texting me and will *not* get a clue, Nora and Charlie will be here any minute, Slay will be here in less than an hour, I haven't done my hair or makeup, and I'm completely in over my head!" She scraped her hands through her hair and tugged in frustration.

Tess stood and walked over to put her arm around Alice's shoulders. "Sweetie, we've got this. I brought my whole makeup kit, Heidi brought the dress and shoes, and Hillie's really good with hair. We'll have you ready in two minutes."

Hillary stood and dragged her chair over to place it in front of Alice's full-length mirror, then gently pushed Alice into it. With deft hands, she scooped and twisted Alice's long, blonde hair into a casual but elegant coil. Heidi procured a handful of hair pins from Alice's dresser and held them out to Hillary so that she could secure the style.

A moment later, Alice twisted her head back and forth, and her eyes widened. "That looks… perfect."

Hillary shrugged, pleased. "No problem, babe. You've got awesome hair."

"Okay, I'm not as fast as Hillie, but hold still and I'll be done in a few minutes," Tess said, stepping between Alice and the mirror to work her magic with the cosmetics.

"So, while Tess does her thing," Heidi said, leaning her back against Alice's dresser. "Why don't you tell us why you're *really* freaking out."

Alice blinked. "I told you, I'm running late, and I…"

"We've all been there," Hillary interrupted, and Tess nodded seriously. "The early days of a serious relationship can be so overwhelming, especially for a submissive, and nobody knows that better than we do. It sometimes helps to know you can talk about it."

Alice sighed and felt her shoulders slump.

"It *is* overwhelming," she admitted. "The whole *trust* thing, you know?"

Heidi nodded. "Boy, do I ever. That's the hardest part."

"What made you think it was a *serious* relationship, anyway?" Alice asked Tess, as Tess blended foundation across her forehead. "I just called you and asked to borrow a dress!"

"You asked to borrow a dress because you were going out with *Slay*," Tess corrected.

"Well, yeah…" Alice agreed.

"I remember the way you looked the minute you found out he was shot," Tess whispered. "You looked like your whole world was ending."

Alice remembered it too, and pressed her lips together.

"So I called Heidi and told her you needed *the* dress," Tess said.

"And when she told me, I remembered the way Slay watched you when we were at Charlie's school fair," Heidi said, placing her hand on Alice's shoulder. "Always focused on you, always knowing exactly where you were and who was around you." She smiled. "And I was thrilled, because he's a good guy. And he deserves someone like you."

Alice felt a lump form in her throat. "You think?"

"I *know*," Heidi confirmed. "So I decided I had to bring the dress over myself. And I called Hillie…"

Hillary said, "And I knew I had to come, too."

"Because she loves to collect inspiration for her novel writing," Heidi joked.

Hillary elbowed her sister gently. "*No*. Because I love *Slay*. In a very platonic, brotherly way," she quickly amended. "Slay helped rescue me from, uh, Marauder," she said, with an audible shudder in her voice for the man who had held her against her will *twice*. "And then Matt tried to set me up on that one ill-fated date with him." She snickered. "You know, the very first day I met you, Alice, I could tell that you had feelings for him. And that he had them for you, though he tried to hide it."

"But it *is* a serious relationship, isn't it?" Tess said, bringing the conversation back around. "When one of these guys finally finds the girl he wants, he seems to go for it, no holds barred. It's just the way they do things."

"It is serious," Alice said, looking from one face to the other. "I guess I was the only one who didn't see it coming. I mean, Slay told me he'd been thinking about me for the longest time, and wanted to see if I was the type of girl who'd be on board for a serious, long-term thing. For the last few months, he's been *testing* me."

Hillary rolled her eyes. "Okay, that's probably not the best way he could have put it. But, really, haven't you been doing the same with him? Haven't we *all* done that? We've gotten to know our guys and knew they were the ones for us… sometimes even before they'd figured it out," she said with a rueful smile.

"I suppose. It's just… I haven't had the best luck with guys," Alice admitted as Tess applied some blush to her cheeks. "The one guy I was serious about before this was Charlie's dad, and when he found out I was pregnant, he left me high and dry. My mom keeps trying to set me up with guys from her church, but the only one who's been interested is this slimeball who won't stop texting me even though I don't reply, and would probably faint if I told him I work at The Club and like to be spanked. So… I dunno. It's hard to believe that things with Slay are real. I just keep waiting for the other shoe to drop, to see his major flaw. And I know it's wrong, so I'm trying to trust him. It's just… hard."

Tess nodded. "I get it. I really do. The way I was raised, I figured a man as kind and talented and *good* as Tony would've been out of my reach forever. It was hard to believe that he was mine."

"And Matteo wanted to keep our relationship platonic for the longest time," Hillary put in. "I really thought he'd never come around."

Alice blew out a breath. "But it seemed to work out well for all of you, right? You just trusted your guys, and everything was fine?" she asked hopefully.

Hillary gave a wide-eyed look to Heidi and then to Tess. "Er… Yeah, something like that," she hedged.

"There were some hairy moments," Tess admitted as she stepped back and snapped her eyeshadow case shut.

"But it all worked out," Heidi soothed.

Alice opened her mouth to ask for more details when they all heard the sound of the lock in the front door, followed by a rumble that could have come from a herd of stampeding buffalo. She heard Charlie call, "We're home, we're home, we're home!"

She shook her head and yelled, "Charles Murray Cavanaugh! Shoes off at the door and no stomping!"

"All right, Momma!" he called back.

Heidi smiled. "Being a mom adds a whole other level to everything, huh?"

"I'm glad Tony and I are planning to wait another year or two before we think about kids," Tess told them.

Hillary pursed her lips and started to say something, but stopped herself.

Charlie careened into the room, ran over to where Alice was sitting, and threw his arms around her for a quick hug.

"You look… *fancy*," he decided when he pulled back.

"Thank you. How was drawing club?" she asked.

"Good! Mrs. O'Gara said that we could draw whatever we wanted, so I drew Beast from the X-Men for Slay, because he kinda reminds me of Beast."

Alice blinked. "The, um, blue guy with the fur? Reminds you of Slay?"

"Yeah," Charlie confirmed.

Hillary turned a snicker into a credible imitation of a cough, and Tess turned her head away, likely to hide her smile, but Alice nodded solemnly. "I'm sure he'll love it," she said seriously.

Charlie's smiling was blinding. "Cool!" he said.

"Hey." Nora walked into the room, blonde hair swinging behind her, and smiled at each of the ladies. Her eyes caught on her sister, who was busy sorting through lipglosses. "Tess, can I talk to you for a minute? I could really use some advice." She nodded towards the hallway.

"We can help if you want," Hillary offered with a wide smile, gesturing from herself to Heidi to Alice. "We're great with advice, too."

"Uh…" Nora looked at Alice, hesitated, then nodded. "Okay."

Alice turned to her son. "Charlie, honey, you can go and watch an episode of X-men, and then Nora will come play with you, okay?"

"Awesome!" he breathed, running out of the room before she could change her mind. Alice chuckled.

"Okay, spill," Tess told her sister.

Nora licked her lips and darted another nervous glance at Alice. "Okay, so there's this girl I know. And she, um, is dating a guy who seems like a nice guy. The problem is, her guy has a very, *extremely* questionable associate."

Heidi's forehead wrinkled. "Define *very, extremely questionable*."

"Like, the associate is a criminal and a thief and a drug dealer, *that* kind of very, extremely questionable," Nora said.

"Yikes," Hillie breathed.

"Wait, are you talking about Mom's old boyfriend, Roger? Is he hanging around her again?" Tess asked, dabbing a final bit of gloss on Tess's lips before putting her makeup away and zipping up her bag. Alice knew that Tess's and Nora's mom had been dating an asshole who had attempted to level-up from a small-time thief to a big-time criminal, and had gotten Nora kidnapped in the process, but they'd all thought he'd left town weeks before.

"I have no idea if Roger's around," Nora said, shaking her head. "I haven't seen Mom in a month, and I don't even talk to her on the phone." Alice noted that Nora didn't seem very upset about that, either.

"So, wait, your friend is dating a guy, and that guy is friends with a drug-dealing criminal?" Heidi repeated. "Does the guy *know* he's hanging out with a criminal?"

Nora nodded slowly. "Evidence would, um, suggest that he does, yes."

"And does your friend know that her guy is hanging out with a criminal?" Alice asked distractedly.

She stood up and took stock of her appearance in the mirror. *Damn.* Tess had somehow managed to do a smoky-eye thing without making Alice look like she had two black eyes. She looked pretty darn good, if she did say so herself.

"Uh, no. I can say pretty confidently that she *doesn't* know," Nora said.

"Hmm," Alice said. "Well, then you need to tell her."

"Agreed," Heidi said. "If your friendship is close enough that you can tell her the hard stuff like that."

But Tess had been watching Nora closely and she seemed to come to a realization. She closed her eyes for a moment as if praying for patience. "Actually, I think before you tell your friend anything, you should check your facts," she said pointedly. "Like, are you *sure* her guy is hanging out with a criminal?

Not just, say, bumping into him on the street and being polite?"

"Yes," Nora said, raising her chin defiantly. "Don't treat me like I'm a little kid who's imagining things, Tess. He is not the nice guy you think he is! It's a *fact*."

Tess shook her head impatiently. "Nor, honest to God, you need to let this go."

"I can't!" Nora argued.

"You *won't*," Tess said. "I have had this conversation with you a million times. *Tony* has had this conversation with you at least *half* a million times. He saved your life."

"You weren't there, Tess," Nora argued. "You don't know how it was!"

"No, I know I don't, honey," Tess said, throwing her hands up in frustration. "And I'm not saying you should forget it, or that you shouldn't talk to your therapist about it, or that you have to be best friends with this guy and invite him over for dinner. I'm not even saying that he's a good guy, although any guy who helped rescue you can't be *all* bad, as far as I'm concerned. But I'm telling you that you need to stop obsessing about him, for your own safety!"

"Who are you two talking about?" Heidi demanded.

"Diego," Nora said flatly, ignoring her sister's glare. "Diego Santiago."

Heidi looked blankly from Hillary to Alice to Tess, seeking an explanation. Hillary frowned, as though trying to place the name, but Alice remembered it all too well. She had a sinking feeling in the pit of her stomach as she asked, "Diego? Isn't that the guy who brought Nora home after she was kidnapped? The one who's friendly with… Slay?"

"That's the guy," Tess confirmed wearily. "Nora believes he works for Salazar, the same guy Roger worked for."

"Whoa," Heidi said. "Seriously?"

Nora nodded vehemently. "He *did*. He *does*. Diego hung

around with Salazar and Roger and the other guys *at my mom's house*. I heard them all talking about selling drugs, about *women*, about hurting people," Nora said. "I had to lock myself in the bedroom." Her brown eyes were glazed with remembered fear.

The guy who had told them Slay was shot, who had called Slay by name, worked for a drug dealer? *What*?

"Nora," Tess said soothingly, reaching out a hand, but Nora shook her head.

"When Roger brought me back to Chalo Salazar's warehouse after he'd kidnapped me, Diego was there. He wasn't there to *rescue* me. He was there as one of Salazar's goons. Slay showed up, Roger shot him. Salazar went ballistic on Roger, saying they didn't need this kind of complication, and told Diego to get rid of me. So yeah, Diego brought me home, but only because *Salazar* told him to. If Salazar had decided to keep me, Diego would have gone along with it. I bet he would have *killed* me if Salazar had told him to."

"Honey," Tess said, wrapping an arm around her sister's shoulders while Nora stood stiffly, tears in her eyes.

"Nora, Slay is a good man," Hillary reminded her gently. "I haven't met all of Matt's friends and associates, but between the guys he tattoos, and the guys he's worked security with, the guys he's served with, even the guys he grew up with, he knows a lot of what you might call *questionable* people—people who have made bad choices, sometimes out of desperation, and ended up on the wrong side of the law. I bet Slay knows people like that, too."

Nora looked away and said nothing, so Hillary took a deep breath and plowed on. "But even though they've done questionable things, Matteo doesn't cut that connection because he still cares about them. I don't think that makes *Matteo* a bad person. It's not that black and white. Diego may or may not be a bad guy, but Slay definitely isn't, even if he and Diego are acquainted."

Nora nodded stiffly without meeting Hillary's eyes.

"Nor, I'm more concerned that you're still looking into this Diego guy," Tess said worriedly. "You've been searching for him online; you keep thinking you see him on the street or around campus when you're taking your dual enrollment classes…"

"Because I *do!*" Nora insisted.

Tess continued as if she hadn't heard her. "I don't know what it is about Diego that's got you so obsessed, but you need to stop. Think about it this way, Nor: if he *is* a bad guy, or even a *questionably bad* guy, you're only putting yourself in danger by looking into him."

Nora opened her mouth to argue, then shut it without speaking. "Okay," she said finally.

"Okay?" Tess repeated.

"Yeah, okay." Nora smiled more fully. "You're probably right. I've developed an unhealthy obsession somehow. I'll talk to Margot, my counselor, about it. And I'll drop it."

"You will?" Tess was dubious.

"Totally. Yes. Consider it dropped!" she said brightly. "Hey, Al, I'm gonna go play with Charlie now, okay?"

Alice nodded woodenly and watched as Nora left, and then as Hillary stepped forward to speak to Tess in a low voice. Her chest was tight with a feeling she recognized right away as totally irrational fear… though somehow, knowing it was irrational didn't make it any less real. Hillary was right, of course. Slay knew Diego because they served together or something, and when Nora had been kidnapped, of course Slay had called on any and all resources to get her back, *especially* the ones who might have information on criminals. It didn't mean that they were *tight,* as Nora said. It didn't make *Slay* a criminal, just because he *knew* one.

And yet an insistent voice in the back of her mind wondered whether the rest of the world would see it that way. What would her parents think? What would Charlie think?

Heidi seemed to recognize the panic in Alice's eyes and

placed a comforting hand on Alice's forearm. "This isn't a big deal, honey. Really. You *know* Slay. We all do."

Alice let out the breath she'd been holding. "Right. I know you're right. I'm going to ask him about it, let him explain."

Heidi smiled. "Good! For a second, I thought you might fly off the handle."

Alice nodded. "Even just a couple of weeks ago, I *would* have. But I'm trying really hard here." She gave Heidi a small smile.

"Atta girl," Heidi said, wrapping her arms around Alice in an impulsive hug.

Then, turning to Hillary and Tess, she continued, "All right, glam squad. I think it's time for us to pack up and get out of here before Slay shows up and sees us all standing around gawking. And I told Dom I'd be home on time."

"Not to mention, it's nearly dinner!" Hillary pointed out. "I'm ravenous."

Tess rolled her eyes. "I think you have a hollow leg, Tinker Bell. But if you want, we can stop by *Cara* on the—"

"Yes!" Hillary cried grabbing Tess's arm excitedly. "Definitely. What do we have on the menu with *capers*?"

"Capers?" Tess looked bewildered. "Wow. That's oddly specific. Um, there's the chicken picatta—"

"Yes, that's what I want. Will Rao make mine with extra capers?" Hillary asked. "And maybe some pepper flakes?"

Tess grabbed her makeup bag and rolled her eyes. "Uh, I'm sure he would. What's gotten into you?" she laughed.

She gave Alice a wink, Hillary kissed her on the cheek, and they were off, leaving Alice with Nora, Charlie, and her thoughts.

Alice had mostly composed herself and had taken on the task of selecting some jewelry to compliment the dress when Nora appeared in the bedroom doorway a little while later.

"Hey, honey," Alice said, holding a pair of dangly earrings against her ear and admiring the look in the mirror. "You okay? I want you to know, I appreciate you saying you'd stay overnight tonight, but if you're too upset, we can—"

"Alice, I don't think you should go out tonight," Nora blurted out, clasping her hands together. "I'll stay if you want me to, but…"

Alice shook her head and turned away from her dresser. "Nora—"

"I didn't tell you guys the whole story," Nora said, walking over to sit down on the edge of the bed facing Alice. "Tess is convinced that I'm *obsessed* with Diego so whenever I tell her the stuff I find out, she comes up with the most random excuses in the book for how I must have misinterpreted things. But I'm *not* obsessed with Diego. I'm just determined to do whatever I can to bring these guys to justice."

"O-okay," Alice agreed, leaning back against her dresser. "But don't you think you should let the police take care of it? Or—"

"The police aren't involved," Nora said hotly. "Not *one* police officer ever came to interview me or anything after I got home."

"What? But why not?" Alice demanded.

"I asked Tony that. He said it was because *Slay* asked them not to. I guess Diego did Slay a favor and tipped him off to where I was being held. Maybe Slay didn't want to get poor *Diego* in trouble by getting the cops involved," she said bitterly. "But in the meantime, there are these criminals, Alice, and they're still doing who-the-hell-knows-what to *other* girls, girls who don't have anyone to come and rescue them. And I can't tell the police what I know because of Slay and his friend Diego."

Alice frowned. *Well. When you put it that way. But…*

"Maybe Slay's trying to protect you, Nor. I mean, if you go to the police, that puts you on Salazar's radar again, right? Right now, you're a blip. A mistake. But if you go poking around…"

Nora rubbed her forehead and sighed in frustration. "But that's *my* decision," she argued. "And believe me, I would choose to go to the police, especially after what I saw today."

A feeling of dread had Alice crossing over to sit on the bed beside Nora.

"What happened?" Alice demanded.

"I went to P&B to pick up Charlie from his drawing lesson. Mrs. O'Gara's room is in the basement, you know?"

Alice nodded.

"I went in the front door of the school, but I went down the stairs on the right side of the building, mostly because the sun was setting and it always looks so pretty with the trees over there? Anyway, when I looked out…" Nora swallowed and knitted her hands together in her lap. "I saw Mindy Freeman sitting in her Suburban in the side parking lot."

Alice nodded in confusion. "Well, right. Her Fiona is in the same drawing class with Charlie, so she—"

"And Chalo Salazar was sitting in the passenger's seat beside her. She did not look pleased."

Alice blinked once, then twice. She didn't want to accuse Nora of falsehood, but this was simply too fantastical to be believed. Mindy Freeman was a bitch of the first water, and if Nora had seen her tripping someone in the hallway or kicking a puppy or cheating on her husband with the gym teacher, Alice would have believed it in a heartbeat. But meeting with a drug kingpin, in her SUV, parked in the lot of a prestigious private school, while waiting for her kid to get out of art class? Mindy wouldn't let anyone *touch* her car unless their pedigree checked out, let alone *sit* inside it.

"How sure are you about this?" Alice asked gently.

"Very, *very* sure," Nora said. "I would recognize those faces anywhere. I see them every night when I close my eyes."

"Faces?" Alice echoed.

Nora nodded. "Diego was standing outside the car. Acting as bodyguard."

Alice licked her lips, tasting the stupid gloss that Tess had smeared there. "Okay. Okay, right. When Slay gets here, you have to tell him."

"I don't know," Nora said dubiously.

"Nora, he'll believe you," Alice said. "He likes you. And he'll look into it and help us get the police involved."

"I know he'll *believe* me, Al," Nora scoffed. "I have photographic evidence."

"You what?"

"I took a picture with my phone," Nora said smugly. "See for yourself."

Nora took out her cell phone and flipped it toward Alice. Sure enough, the image showed a man who looked remarkably like the one who had brought Nora home all those weeks ago standing outside Mindy's gold-colored SUV, while a very pissed-off Mindy sat inside chatting with an older Hispanic man. And in the background were the distinctive ivy-colored red brick walls of Charlie's school.

"My God," Alice breathed. "At Pevrell and Brahms."

"It's a different issue when it hits closer to home, isn't it?" Nora said, not unkindly.

Alice gaped at her.

It *was* different. It really, really was. She wanted Chalo Salazar on a different *planet* from her kid, but at the very least to believe he'd never *heard* of Charlie's school. And what the hell was he doing with Mindy?

"So, yeah, I know Slay will *believe* me," Nora repeated glumly. "I'm just not sure he'll do the right thing, even when he knows."

The doorbell rang, but Alice sat frozen on the bed, Nora's phone in her hand. Nora stood and said, "I'll get it."

When she heard Slay greeting Charlie and heading down the hall, Alice stood mechanically and swallowed.

Keep it together, Cavanaugh.

Of course Slay would do the right thing here. He was a good man. Her *daddy*. She trusted him not only to do what was best for her, but what was *right* and moral. Recognizing the truth of that let the constriction in her chest ease so that she could draw a deep breath.

Slay appeared in her bedroom a moment later, wearing jeans and a light green button-down shirt with his leather jacket. When he spotted her, his caramel eyes widened almost comically before lowering to a half-masted smolder. It was a really good look on him.

"Oh, Allie-girl," he breathed. "What the *hell* are you wearing?"

Alice looked down, so distracted that she was almost surprised to find herself wearing the red dress. She smiled hesitantly. "I borrowed it from Heidi. Do you like it?"

"Baby, I love it," he told her, coming forward to wrap his arms around her waist. "You look fucking amazing." He lowered his head to press an open-mouthed kiss to the side of her neck. "Now hurry up and change so we can get going."

Alice giggled. The dress scored three out of three when it came to turning a dom into a caveman.

But she put one restraining hand on Slay's chest. "Daddy, I really need to talk to you first, okay? It's important."

Slay stepped back so he could meet her eyes squarely, while keeping his hands on her hips. "Of course. What do you need, baby?" he asked.

Alice took a deep breath. *See*? she told herself. *This is all going to be fine.*

"Well, Nora saw something today at Charlie's school that really upset her," Alice began. "She came to me for advice. A- and I think she should go to the police about it."

Slay frowned. "Shit. Something with one of the teachers?" he asked. The concern in his eyes made Alice's heart melt for him just a little bit more.

"No. One of the parents," Alice corrected. "She saw Mindy Freeman sitting in a car with, um, Chalo Salazar."

Slay's whole face closed off, like a switch had been flipped. It was the most bizarre thing. One minute he was right there with her, they were a team, and then suddenly he'd erected a wall between them. Even his eyes were cooler now, and his jaw was set.

"That's crazy," he told her flatly. But the instantaneous denial, coupled with his complete withdrawal, told her that it was anything *but* crazy. And Slay knew it.

"She has proof," Alice whispered, gesturing to the cell phone she still held in her hand.

"Jesus," Slay muttered, releasing her and stepping back. "Show me."

Reluctantly, Alice handed over the cell phone, where the image of Diego standing outside of a car, with Salazar in the front seat, was still displayed in high-resolution. She heard him expel a breath.

"This could be anyone," he declared. "All I see is a dark-haired guy standing outside a car, and an older, heavier guy sitting inside it. Nora needs to stop spooking at shadows."

And then he moved his finger to delete the picture, along with the ones before and after it.

"Slay! What are you doing?" Alice demanded, grabbing at his arm. "Those are Nora's!"

"They're *trouble*, that's what they are," he informed her. He held the cell phone out of her reach, his eyes bright with temper. "Nora needs to keep her head down, to focus on graduating high school and taking her college classes. You got me? And I don't want you encouraging her in her wild goose chase."

"But that's *her* choice to make, isn't it?" Alice asked desperately. "Slay, if she wants to go to the police, we should be supporting her, not—"

"Alice, I have my reasons and I can't share them with you right now. I've given you my decision about this and it's final," he said sternly. "I'm going to go have a word with Nora, but you and I are not discussing this again. Now, find a dress that's not going to get me in a bar fight or a car accident, okay, baby?" And the man had the gall to attempt a smile.

Alice felt her chin drop.

"Are you kidding? Slay, I'm not going anywhere until you've explained things," she said, planting her hands on her hips. "You're telling me to trust you, but you have to give me more information. That was a picture of Diego and Chalo Salazar. If I wasn't sure of it before, I became sure the second you deleted it from Nora's phone without her permission."

Slay's jaw locked. "I *said* we are not getting into this, Allie."

Arrogant man! They were already *in* it! And he was making it a hundred times worse by treating her like a child who wasn't entitled to an explanation!

"Nora said that you told Tony not to have her file a police report after she was abducted," Alice whispered. "Is that true? Why would you do that? Just tell me, please! I want to follow your lead, Slay. I want *so badly* to trust you here…"

Slay laughed without humor and ran a hand over his face. "Do you know what trust means, baby?" he asked in a heated whisper. "Trust means that if I say 'Alice, we're not talking about this right now,' you say 'Okay,' " he told her. "Following my lead means that if I say, 'This is dangerous, you need to stop,' then you fucking *stop*. You don't make me have a goddamn fucking debate with you about all the reasons why I think you need to stop, and why *you* think you *don't* need to stop, and *whatever the fuck else*. That's what *obedience* is. That's what *submission* is. I told you I can't discuss this. *Can't*, Allie, not *won't*. You need to accept that and move on."

"Well, how about if you tell me what *dominance* is then," Alice retorted stung by his words and angered by the impatience in his tone. Did he think that trust came that easily? Just snap her fingers and *poof*? "It doesn't mean you get to just lay down the law, like I'm a person without judgment or feelings. We're supposed to be a team, not—"

"It's about *protection*, Allie. For me, dominance is always about protection."

Because she knew that was true, because she knew that he was somehow misguidedly trying to keep her and Nora and Diego and everyone safe right now, she took a deep breath and let it out slowly, reining in her temper.

"Slay, honey," she said. "This isn't about protecting *me*, it's about Nora, and helping her get justice after everything she's gone through. Please, just try—"

He cut her off with single firm shake of his head. "Allie, I'm already *trying*. Trying to protect you, to support you, to have your back. Have you tried to trust me?"

It always came back to this, didn't it? *Can't* and *won't* was an important distinction when it came to what he'd discuss with her, but apparently not when it came to trusting him. The double standard rankled. He insisted that trust was a choice, and maybe that was true, but she was finding that it wasn't an *easy* choice. Not for her. And he didn't seem to get it.

"I am trying *right now*," she whispered. "I wish you could see that. But the decision you're making here involves a lot of people, and you're not even taking their wishes into consideration. I don't know how I could begin to justify that to Nora."

"Alice, listen to yourself." Slay lifted one hand and rubbed the back of his neck. "If Nora has a problem with me, *she* can come to me. You don't have to justify my decisions to Nora or anyone. You submit to *me*. No one else gets a vote in this, no one else's opinion matters. They think I'm an asshole? Fine. I don't give a shit. You shouldn't give a shit either. You follow my lead because you know it's the right thing to do, and you don't need to convince anyone else."

"I *want* to submit. I just wanted an explanation about this *one little thing*," she said in a small voice.

"Nah, Allie. You're not looking for an *explanation*; you're looking for an *excuse*. A reason to guard yourself from me. And, baby, if you look for an excuse, you'll always find one." Slay crossed his arms over his chest and looked at her sternly. "It all comes down to this: Do you trust me, Alice?"

Alice pressed her lips together and stared at him… at Slay, at her daddy. His caramel eyes were molten hot, his posture rigid, and any idiot could see with one glance that he meant what he said –he would not budge on this, and he would not discuss it. And the entirety of the choices available to her right now seemed to be going along with him, even when she thought he was wrong, or ending things entirely, an idea that, even though they'd been together for such a short time, made her chest constrict so tightly she couldn't breathe.

Was this submission? she wondered bitterly. Still, she had to tell the truth.

"Yeah," she said sullenly. Because she *did* trust Slay. She trusted him with her life and with Charlie's. She trusted him to protect everyone she loved. She just wished that *he* would trust *her* with a little more information. And it hurt that he couldn't see that.

"You'll wanna watch your tone," he warned. "I am on the edge right now, little girl."

She inhaled sharply and clenched her fists together, for the first time *feeling* like a little girl in a way that was not remotely pleasant. Slay wasn't the only one on the edge.

God, this was hard.

"I trust you," she ground out.

He nodded once, and she could swear she saw something like relief flit across his face before he hardened his jaw again. The thought crossed her mind that maybe this wasn't as easy for him as it seemed, either. She filed that away to think about later.

"So I'm going to say this exactly one more time, Allie, before I lock this door and haul you over my lap. *Go get changed.*"

She took a deep breath. "Fine," she said with narrowed eyes. "I'll change."

She spun around to face her closet, but his silky voice had her stopping in her tracks.

"Pardon?" he said. "Is that how you speak to me?"

Oh, he was not gonna push this right now, was he? When he'd already won? She turned around to face him, incredulous, and felt hot tears come to her eyes.

"What do you call me, Alice?" he pressed softly, seriously, like the answer was vitally important to him.

So many names were coming to mind right now, names that would get her ass whipped if she spoke even the first syllable aloud, and she could tell by the glint in his eye that he knew it, too.

He stalked toward her and wrapped one hand around the back of her neck, tilting her face back so that she could look up, up, up at him as he towered over her. Then he lowered his head until their breath was mingling and their lips just barely touching.

"Tell me, Allie," his voice a low purr against her skin. "What do you call me?"

She swallowed hard, her heart beating a mile a minute, her breath stuck in her throat. She had good reasons to be angry. Very good reasons. But they seemed to burn off temporarily under the wave of excitement that swamped her.

"D-daddy," she said softly. "I call you Daddy."

He leaned fractionally closer and took her bottom lip firmly between his teeth. She felt her core go liquid. *God, this man.*

"That's right, baby. You do." He squeezed her hip with his free hand. "And I swear to God, Allie, I will do whatever I have to do so that you never regret calling me that," he told her. His hand moved from her hip, down the short skirt of her dress to flirt with the hem. "I get you find this shit hard for whatever reason, but you did the right thing today, baby. Trust your man, yeah? Simple as that."

"Okay, Daddy," she agreed, her attention focused on his fingers as they trailed up her thigh beneath her skirt to toy with the lace-edged silk of her panties.

She noted that Slay was breathing hard, too, and his eyes, as they stared into hers, were unfocused. He stepped back sharply.

"Get changed, Allie-girl," he said, his voice choked and husky. "Now. Or this will be the shortest date in history, and we won't ever leave the house."

And despite everything, Alice giggled. The dress was working its magic again.

Chapter 8

S lay usually was pretty damn good at handling tension, challenging situations, high intensity. As a Marine, he'd dedicated his fucking *life* to protecting others first. Duty to country trumped all else. He'd pulled brothers out of burning buildings overseas, and once saved a drowning man from a riptide in the ocean, hauling his ass to safety. He commanded the men under him, and always reminded them of the motto that fueled the blood of every brother in his battalion.

Death before dishonor.

He'd fight to the death to protect the innocent. From a very young age, he'd accepted the fact that he'd been gifted with an exceptionally strong body, razor-sharp instincts, and tenacious self control. When he'd grown of age, it was only natural he join the Marines and devote his life to the most dangerous missions any man in uniform faced. He could still recite the decades-old lines he'd learned when promoted to drill sergeant.

I will train them to the best of my ability. I will develop them into smartly disciplined, physically fit, basically trained Marines, thoroughly indoctrinated in love of Corps and country. I will demand of them, and demonstrate by my own example, the highest standards of personal conduct, morality, and professional skill.

Demonstrate by my own example...

The words rang through his mind when he went to bed at night and when he rose. It was his creed. His motto. His prayer.

Answering the call of duty to his country and military brothers was instinctive as breathing, and it was a natural progression to become a bouncer at Club Black Box. He was a dominant, after all, comfortable only when those in command under him obeyed his commands, reveling in the control he craved. But when it became clear to him that Black Box wasn't interested in enforcing consensual dom-sub play, when their lax rules had led to Hillary being abused by a psychopath masquerading as a dominant, he'd left in favor of the cleaner, more respectable play at The Club.

All his life, he'd faced fear head on, and expected those in command under him to do the same. His women had been no exception. He'd had good reasons for why he'd taken so fucking long to pursue Alice. He couldn't handle a submissive who was in it for roleplay or kink. The power exchange was a vital element to him. He *needed* to be obeyed.

"Where are we going, Daddy?" Alice asked, running her hands along her thighs, clad in the leggings he'd picked out for her. She'd been reluctant to take the dress off. He'd helped her see it was worthwhile removing her clothing when he commanded it. She'd finally emerged from her room, cheeks flushed and eyes bright, wearing black leggings and a fitted, tunic-length sweater in a blue-gray that accentuated her golden hair and blue eyes. She looked *gorgeous*.

"I could buy a burka if you'd like," she'd teased, to which he'd responded by spinning her around by her elbow and swatting her good and hard before ordering her ass to his truck.

She was trying. God, she was trying, and it *killed* him that he couldn't tell her about the undercover operation that could mean *everything.* The timing wasn't right for him to fill her in on anything, not when lives depended on his silence. Eventually, she would know. She would see that it was all about her and Charlie's protection from the very beginning. But until then… until then, so much lay in the balance between them.

Tonight, he'd have to show his little girl how good it was when she obeyed her daddy.

"What's your favorite thing to eat, baby?" he asked, running a hand over the thin leggings, to her upper thighs, until his hand rested just below the edge of her top.

"What?" she breathed.

He lifted his hand and delivered a sharp swat to her inner thigh.

"Little girls listen to their daddies when spoken to."

She gasped, but then she shifted closer to him and her legs spread wider as he ran one finger over her thigh, traveling higher up until he reached between her legs. He could feel her damp with arousal straight through her leggings, and his cock hardened as he pressed a finger to her. She began to pant.

"I said what's your favorite thing to eat, baby?"

"Sushi. I love sushi. It's my favorite thing *ever.*"

Seriously?

"But I love burgers, too. Big, fat, juicy burgers loaded with cheese and bacon, with crispy fries."

He chuckled, still fingering her through the thin fabric. His mind traveled to dark, dirty thoughts as he imagined her licking the salt off her fingers, the back of her hand wiping her mouth clean from the food. She was on her knees, naked, her hands tied behind her back and eyes covered by the silky folds of a blindfold as she took him in her mouth. He'd flick her ass with the tail end of a whip, making her jump and moan, sucking him harder.

He swallowed.

"Burgers or sushi. All right, baby." His mind started turning over the local establishments that would have the best goddamn burger or sushi she'd ever put in her mouth. Because if she was going to put anything in her mouth, it'd better be—

Shit. He was like a fucking teenager.

"They'll all be crowded," Alice murmured, her hand resting atop his on her thigh. She was whispering, moving even closer to him. "We'll have to wait everywhere we go. And there will be *people* everywhere. Crowds, Slay." She looked out the window, pulled a piece of her hair into her mouth with her right hand and chewed thoughtfully as he cruised to a stop at a red light.

He removed his hand from her thigh and reached for her neck, squeezing gently. "You don't like crowds, baby?"

She shook her head and looked over at him. Her eyes were suggestive and coy, half-lidded. "I want to be alone with you," she said. "We have the night to ourselves, and a baby-sitter. I don't have to be home until the morning. And I've… been thinking about that room of yours." She paused, swallowed and her voice dropped to a whisper. "What do you think about take-out, Daddy?"

Hearing the word *daddy* from her, with those fetching blue eyes looking at him suggestively, made his cock surge and his stomach clench. *Fuck.*

"You don't want me to take you on a date?" he asked. His plan had been to wine and dine her, treat her to the best dinner she'd ever had out, complete with whatever she liked to drink, and dessert, and whatever her heart desired. He wanted to spoil her rotten. And she wanted to go back to his place?

"Someday, Slay," she said. "Someday I'd like to go on a date. But tonight? I want to be alone with you." She put her hand on *his* leg as she pleaded. "Please, Daddy. Take me back to your place. Just the two of us."

He didn't need to be asked again. "Consider it done," he growled, his truck gunning to life as the light turned green.

He wouldn't spoil her with food and drink and a fancy restaurant, then. No.

There were many ways daddies could spoil their little girls.

———

He wanted to pick her up and *carry* her up his stairs, he was that eager to get her alone, but he dutifully opened the passenger door, helped her out, and took her hand as they made their way to the building entrance. He watched her flitting up the stairs next to him, light as fairy dust, bouncing on the tips of her toes as he opened the door to his building.

Thankfully, the stairway was empty, and they made it to his place without any further interruptions. He'd unleashed her inner girl, and she was eager. Oh, they were gonna have fun tonight. The second the door shut behind them, he tossed the keys on the counter, spun her around and pushed her up against the door. Both of her hands in his, he lifted them up over her head, pinning them in place as his mouth met hers. Her body yielded to him as he overpowered her, their mouths moving in unison, him taking what was his and Alice gracefully responding to his touch. He pulled away, looking into her eyes, both of them panting.

"I never knew," she said. "All that time I spent at The Club fantasizing about you, and I didn't know how amazing it would feel…"

Fantasizing about him? He lifted her straight up off the ground and her legs entwined his waist. She was a curvy, full-figured woman in every sense of the word and he *loved* the feel of her voluptuous thighs wrapped around him, her full breasts pressed up against his chest as he kissed her, her ass cradled in her hands. Utter fucking perfection. He was a big guy, needed a girl who could take him, and *fuck* but his girl could take him. They kissed as he stomped over to his couch, turned and sat heavily, taking her with him, straddling his lap.

"Ohh, Daddy," she moaned as he pulled away from the kiss.

"Food, baby," he said. "We've got to get you some food."

But her eyes were on fire. She leaned into him. "No," she breathed, both hands flat on his chest. "I don't care about food. Don't stop!"

He easily flipped her over and planted her face-down over his lap. She squealed as he lifted her top and hauled down her leggings, nothing between them now but a thin strip of a light pink thong. He gave her a good, hard swat.

"No arguing, little girl" he scolded. *Crack!* "You don't say no to Daddy, and you don't talk back." Another hard swat hit her thighs and she squealed, then moaned, arching her back and wiggling against his hard cock. He plunged a finger in her core, pumping with a wicked grin as he felt her slick arousal. She moaned even louder. He removed his finger and lifted his hand, bringing it down with another hard swat.

"Do you argue with Daddy?" *Swat!*

She shook her head. "No, sir! I mean, no Daddy!"

Swat!

Fingering her one last second, he finally reluctantly pulled his hands away and pulled her pants up over her reddened ass. He stifled a groan. Lifting her, he positioned her so that she was straddling his lap once again. His hands lowered to her breasts and he pinched her nipples simultaneously. She gasped as her head flew back. "Ohhh. Torture!"

He chuckled darkly, reached for her hair, and pulled her toward him, bringing her mouth to his with a hard kiss before he pulled away.

"What do you want to eat?"

She swallowed. "*You*, Daddy. I want your cock in my mouth."

Fuck.

He closed his briefly eyes and swallowed. "Alice," he warned.

"Yes?" she said as he opened his eyes and looked at her. She blinked innocently.

He tugged her hair. "Be a good girl."

She sighed and her lower lip protruded a bit.

Another tug. "Are you pouting, young lady?"

Her shoulders dropped. God, she was so fucking adorable. "Okay." She took a deep breath and sat up straighter. "All righty then. Food. What's the fastest food in Boston?"

He grinned. "I've got some ideas," he said. "But first, I want to make sure you're prepared while we wait for our food. Stand, Allie-girl."

She pushed off his lap and stood in front of him with wide, expectant eyes.

"Strip, honey."

Her eyes looked down as she grasped the edge of her top and pulled it up, revealing her curvy belly, then the lace-edged lining of a black bra that barely covered her gorgeous breasts.

"Jesus," he swore, as she lifted her top over her head, her golden hair cascading about her shoulders as she whipped the top to the edge of the couch. Next, she shimmied out of her leggings. Now he could see the curve of her hips, her full thighs and delectable, spankable ass as she bent over to toss the leggings on the couch. She stood in nothing but her bra and panties, and her hands instinctively crossed over her belly.

"No covering, baby," he ordered gently.

"But—" she froze, as if suddenly realizing she was about to talk back again. He pursed his lips and gave her a stern look. Obediently, she dropped her hands.

"Come here, Alice," he ordered. Shyly, she stepped toward him. When she was right in front of him, he reached a hand to her shoulder and gently stroked down her arm, then up again. She shivered. "So beautiful," he said. "My girl, so beautiful."

She giggled and opened her mouth to speak but he put a large finger on her lips.

"Hush, now, honey," he said. "Daddy needs to order some food. You'll kneel here, and think about submitting to Daddy. What that will mean from you. What I expect of you. And while you kneel here, you clear your mind. Just focus on doing what I say. Understood?"

She nodded.

His voice deepened and he pointed to the floor. "Kneel."

She dropped to her knees in front of him. He took her hands and placed them together behind her back. "Keep your hands here. I need to grab my phone. You are not to get up from this position. If you get up, or unclasp your hands, my belt comes off. You understand?"

She nodded. Her cheeks were flushed, her eyes bright. "Yes, Daddy."

He placed a hand atop her head, drew her closer and kissed her forehead. "Good girl."

Standing, he retrieved his phone and watched her out of the corner of his eye to make sure she obeyed. She turned her head to look at him and he put his fingers to his lips, kissed, then blew her the kiss across the room as he dialed. She grinned, opened her mouth, pretended to swallow, and licked her lips. He chuckled. As he waited on hold, he watched her. At one point, she wavered, unclasped her hands and readjusted herself, tugging on her bra then letting go and clasping her hands again.

Really, little girl? You think Daddy's joking?

Oh, that wouldn't do. He'd told her what he'd do if she got out of position.

He placed his order. Shutting his phone off, he stalked over to her slowly, watching as her eyes roved his body.

"I've never seen you dressed like this," she said. "Dressed up. Gosh, it's… amazing."

Though he'd removed his jacket, he was still dressed in a button-down shirt and slacks. Ah. She liked the look. His hands went to his wrists and he unbuttoned first one cuff, then the other, rolling each sleeve up to his elbow. He leaned against the back of the couch, eyeing her nearly-naked form on the floor in front of him, and crossed his arms. Her eyes widened, her mouth parted just a tiny bit. Pushing himself off the couch, he stalked over to her and bent down, grasping a handful of hair and pulling her close.

He whispered in her ear. "Food will be here in thirty minutes, little girl. Do you think Daddy has enough time to eat you out?"

She closed her eyes. "*Three* minutes would be enough," she moaned. He chuckled, lowering his hands to her bra strap and unfastening the clasp. As the bra fell to the floor, her breasts swung free and his cock tightened. Shit. He dipped his head, bending low, his tongue flicking against her nipple. She gasped, then he bit down, just enough to make her squeal but not enough that he left more than a tiny red mark. He pinched the other nipple with his thumb and index finger and twisted gently as his tongue circled her left nipple. Her knees wobbled and her hands unclasped but she righted herself.

He pulled his mouth away from her breasts, pulling her head back. "Keep those hands where I put them," he clipped. And he meant it. She'd do exactly as she was told, every fucking instruction. Quickly, her hands went behind her back and clasped again. He dropped to his knees, rewarding her by dipping his mouth to her collarbone and kissing before he nipped her sensitive skin with his teeth. She shifted but stayed in position. Heat rose on her chest, bright pink, as her nipples hardened. He dipped his hand between her legs, pushed her thighs apart, pulled her panties down, and plunged his finger into her core.

"God, baby," he growled in her ear as he fingered her. "You're sopping. So fucking wet for Daddy."

She whimpered as he pumped his finger in and out.

"You're gonna come for me, little one," he whispered in her ear as he continued to finger her. "Daddy's gonna eat you out. But we've got some business to attend to, first, little girl," he said soberly.

Fear flicked across her features. "What's that?" she whispered.

"Daddy's gonna ask you a question, and I expect an honest

answer. Did you or did you *not* keep your hands clasped when I placed the food order?"

Her eyes shifted away from him.

Grasping her chin, he held on tightly. "Eyes to me," he ordered.

She looked back at him and nodded. "I… didn't keep my hands this way the *whole* time," she admitted.

It wasn't a major infraction. It was hard to maintain her position and he well knew it. But he also knew that a good spanking would arouse her and make her climax harder.

Still holding her chin, he nodded. "That's what I thought," he said. "Seems a good spanking is what's in order, young lady," he chided, intentionally speaking sternly and fixing her with a look of admonishment. "Step out of your panties, and hand them to me."

She stood, trembling, stepped out of her panties, and handed them over. He put the small strip of fabric in his pocket. He kept his gaze on her as he unclasped his belt. "What happens to little girls who disobey their daddies?" he asked, pulling the leather through the fabric with a soft *whoosh* before doubling it over. Her eyes were wide as saucers.

"They get spanked," she whispered.

He furrowed his brow at her and pointed to the couch. "That's right. I want you bent over the arm of the couch, toes on the floor, hands flat down in front of you. Understand me?"

She nodded, stepping over to the arm of the couch. He stood behind her and watched as she draped her naked body over the edge, obediently placing both feet on the floor as her hands splayed out on the sofa cushion.

"When Daddy give you an instruction, you're expected to obey," he said, and without another word, he pulled back the doubled-over belt and snapped it against her naked backside. She rose to the tips of her toes and gasped. As a reddened stripe rose on her bottom, his cock strained for release. He reared back and let loose another snap of the belt. He could easily modulate the swing of his shortened belt, especially when she was lying over the couch. He would leave her bottom stinging and warm to the touch, but not welted or bruised.

He let loose six swats, one after the other, as he lectured her about obeying. "You'll obey Daddy." *Whap!* "You will do as you're told." *Whap!* "It's hard for you to trust, but you're doing so well, baby girl." *Whap!* She gasped as the leather belt wrapped around her upper thighs, but he kept spanking. "You told the truth when asked, so your spanking won't be as hard as it could be." Another hard swat fell, but then he was done. If she'd lied on top of it, he would've moved on to a good paddling, but for now, she would be repentant and submissive. She'd also be fucking wet for him.

"You stay right there, little girl," he said, threading his belt back through the loops of his pants and fastening the buckle. He stepped up to her and ran his hand over her warmed ass. "Such a good girl for Daddy," he soothed, rubbing out the sting. Her honey glistened between her legs and bare mound. He dipped a finger in her wetness.

"Turn around," he ordered. She turned to face him, eyes wide and obedient. She gingerly sat on the edge of the arm, bracing herself so that her pink pussy faced him. He knelt in front of her, gently spreading her legs. "That's a girl," he whispered, his tongue flicking out and lapping at her clit. "Such a good girl," he murmured between strokes of his tongue. "My very good girl." He sucked on her clit and her hips jerked, then he leisurely circled, alternating sucks and flicks of his tongue, stroking upward until he felt her trembling, just the right amount of pressure. Her breath was coming in gasps now, and she was on the verge of climax, her grasp so tight on the edge of the couch her knuckles were white. He pulled away.

"Take what's yours, baby."

She moaned at the command, her head thrown back. He pumped his fingers in her core as he drew close again. His tongue circled her clit. She whimpered, ready, on the verge of climax.

"Come on Daddy's face, babygirl," he ordered, his voice thick with arousal. He dipped his head back to her pussy, pumped hard with his fingers as he flicked his tongue. Seconds later she was moaning, her hips rising as she came, her head thrown back with abandon, the sexiest fucking thing he'd ever seen. He pumped and licked, stroking her to completion until she collapsed against him and the couch.

He chuckled as he came to the front of the couch. Her eyes were shut, her chest heaving, and as he sat down she pounced on him, wrapping her legs around his body and her arms around his neck. She clung to him as he held her tight. Her eyes stayed shut, her head on his chest, as he smoothed the soft blonde hair splayed against the fabric of his light green shirt.

"That's my good girl," he whispered. "Daddy's very good girl." He glanced at the clock on the entertainment center. A thorough spanking followed by a hard climax would leave her clinging to him, divested of whatever had been on her mind, and he was fully prepared to give her the time and attention she needed.

Glancing to the side, he saw the door to his office. He'd give her everything she needed… except the truth. She couldn't get the *whole* truth from him. Not yet.

Slay opened his door and handed the delivery guy cash, as Alice roamed his playroom with permission. He liked the idea of doing a totally normal thing like paying for takeout, while his naked submissive was just in the other room ogling his wares. He'd unlocked the door and told her to check things out, see what interested in her, and he'd meet her in there shortly.

"Alice," he called, after he'd paid. "Come here."

She came to him, her arms crossed on her chest self-consciously. They'd work on that. "Oh, that smells *so* good. May I please put some clothes on?"

He quirked a brow. "Absolutely not. Why would you do a thing like that?" He tried his best to look serious, but it was hard to stay focused. He wanted to push her up against the wall and fuck her hard right here and now.

"Um, sanitary reasons? I'm not really comfortable with sitting my very tender spanked ass on your kitchen chair." She crossed her arms over her naked breasts.

"Who said you were sitting on a chair?" he said, pulling a chair out and sitting down. He patted his lap. Smiling shyly, she walked over to him. "On my knee, baby," he said in his deep voice.

She obediently sat down. "That's a good girl," he said, his hand on her soft belly, he adjusted her on his lap, and flicked open the lids to the burgers, fries, and salad he'd ordered.

"Mmm," she said. "Ohh, this looks so good."

"Help yourself, honey," he said. It felt so damn good to have her on his lap. He was pleased to see she didn't need to be asked twice, as she snagged the food and began to eat.

"So, tell me what you think of the room," he said. "Anything you want to try? Anything you *don't* want to?"

"Well," she said, squirming on his lap. "Honestly, the… um, post looks interesting. I've never been stretched out and whipped, but you spank hard so I'm not so sure I'd like that."

He swallowed a fry. "Doesn't have to be a whip, baby. I'm happy to use a flogger. Some are tame, almost tickle."

She nodded. It wouldn't be all about what she liked. If she earned a punishment, it wouldn't be fun for either of them. Still, he needed to know what *did* appeal to her.

"The spanking bench also has me curious. I checked out the implements, too. I'm curious about… well, most of them, to be honest. The clamps for sure are intriguing. I've had some sessions at The Club, but… that was different."

Sure as hell it was different.

"The restraints look interesting, but…" she put a fry down and looked away. Her face had gone pale, and the humor that had been dancing in her eyes evaporated.

"What, honey?" he said, concerned about the shift.

"No blindfolds, Daddy," she whispered. "Remember? Please?"

He'd been fantasizing about tying a silky blindfold over her eyes, and using the deprived sense of sight to heighten the session. "It's okay," he said. "I do like the idea of blindfolding you and ramping you up that way. It shows you trust me. But I get that you don't want to go there. Can you tell me why, honey?"

"I don't know," she said. "It scares me. It's even… it's a hard limit, Slay. I can't do it. I don't *want* to do it," she said now, in a rush of words that concerned him. She was afraid. "I don't like the idea of not being able to see. I'm trying hard to trust you, I really am. But I need to know I have some control here."

Ah. Control. It was at the very crux of everything they did. The give and take of power, the give and take of trust. It was where she'd find her ultimate fulfillment. But they'd have to work to get there.

He'd fucked up, and he was still learning himself.

"Maybe you need to experience something you're afraid of so you can learn to trust me," he suggested.

Her eyes hardened, her lips pursed. "Or maybe *you* need to listen to me when I tell you I have a hard limit," she snapped.

His response was instinctive. He pulled her hair back and pulled her ear to his mouth. "I'm listening, Allie. There's no need to be rude. We're talking. But I don't want you to talk to me that way again. Got it?"

"Yes, Daddy," she whispered, nodding her head as best she

could with his hand grasping her hair.

"Good." He kissed her forehead. "I get it. I'll respect your limits. Just don't stop talking to me. You get me?"

Her eyes softened and she nodded. "I do," she said.

He released her, balled up the napkins, and stacked everything together. "If you need to freshen up in the bathroom, do that now. Then I'll meet you in the room. When I come in there, I want you kneeling on the bench, belly down, ready for Daddy. Yeah?"

She nodded. "Yes, Daddy."

He sent her off with a swat to the ass that had her squealing, as he quickly tidied his kitchen. When he joined her a few minutes later, she was obediently on the bench as instructed. It was a sight he could get used to. Her breasts pushed up against the padded leather, her belly down, ass in the air, presenting to him.

"Very good," he murmured, coming up behind her and running his hand along the small of her back, the roughness of his hand smoothing over her bare skin. "Such a good girl."

"What's behind the locked door, Daddy?" she asked.

He froze. It was the last thing he expected to hear.

"That's private," he said.

He could see the visible tension as she tilted her head to the side. "We're doing that again?"

Without thinking he smacked his hand down on her naked backside.

She yelped and frowned. "Why did you spank me?"

"You're being rude again," he said.

"But I was only asking!"

He was half tempted to give her another swat, but appreciated how difficult this was for her. "I told you there were some things I had to hold onto for now," he said. "Yeah, it's private, and yeah, I can't tell you about it now." He paused, rubbing her naked skin. "But I want you to trust me, Alice." He sighed. What else could he do to show her that it was for her own good? That not knowing right now was in her best interest? Not only could her knowing put Diego at risk, it could put *her* at risk.

She closed her eyes and inhaled. When she opened them, she looked determined. "Okay," she said. "All right, Daddy. This is what I'm doing. You've got me naked, sprawled out on a bench, ready to take whatever you give me. I'm not going to ask questions about the room. I'm going to do my very best to…" she paused, inhaled, then exhaled, "*trust* you. My very best. I promise."

He nodded. It was the best he could ask from her. He walked over to the table and took her wrists in his hand, bending down to kiss each one before placing her hands in the restraints attached to the bench and cinching.

"Too tight?" he asked.

"No, Daddy."

He nodded. She was already breathing in low gasps, as he gently pulled one ankle, then the other into the stirrups at the base of the bench. He fastened the leather cuffs that held her in place, and gently moved her until she was in the exact position he wanted her in, spread eagle and ready, her gorgeous ass on display and ready to take whatever he gave her. God, he wanted to pull his cock out and take her, right here, right now. He reached out and ran his hand over her hair, smoothing it back from her forehead and neck. Bending, he planted a kiss to her neck.

"I know you said no blindfold, honey," he whispered. "I want you to close your eyes when you can, and try to get to that place of letting go. That way you can open your eyes if you need to. You get me?"

"Yes, Daddy," she said, nodding, as much as she could with her cheek pressed up against the leather.

He'd placed a variety of implements on pegs on the wall near the bench. Selecting a sturdy paddle, he walked back over to her.

Her eyes followed him the whole way, until he came up behind her and placed a hand on her lower back. "Relax, little girl. Relax and trust Daddy."

He lifted the paddle and brought it down with a sharp but moderate crack. The breath hissed out of her and her skin turned pink. Again, he swatted her with the paddle, slowly bringing the heat to the surface of her skin, warming her up good so she could take whatever he gave her. Swat after swat fell, and at first she flinched with each stinging stroke, but after a few more, he saw the tension leave her body. She no longer flinched with each spank but now slumped against the table. Good. Very good. She was warmed up. Switching the paddle to his left hand, he stroked her naked bottom, and she moaned. He walked back over to the pegs, hung the paddle back up, and removed a thin bamboo rod.

Her eyes were shut as he walked back over to her and again, placed a hand on her back as he snapped the cane against her pink skin. She jumped a bit, but the swat was again moderate. He peppered her backside evenly, painting her all over with little flicks of the cane. Stripes rose against her skin, but still, she took it.

"So good," he whispered to her ear. "Such a good girl. Taking her spanking like a very good girl." Though her eyes stayed closed, her lips turned up in a smile. He placed the cane back and removed a long, thick leather strap. He wanted her to fully succumb to his power, to submerge herself in the spanking. Over time, he'd be able to bring her to sub-space with the varied spanking techniques, a good, long session with varying intensity a good gateway to bliss for the trained submissive. It would likely take time to get there. Her eyes fluttered open as he walked back over to her with the strap, but quickly shut again. He grinned. She was trying. His sweet girl was trying.

"Such a good girl," he whispered, as he reared back and snapped the strap against her vulnerable backside. She flinched and yelped, but he kept going, landing one good swat after another. She shrieked.

"Ow, Daddy! Oh, that hurts so much!"

But he didn't stop, not until he'd delivered three more rapid, stinging swats. When he stopped, she slumped against the table again. It was necessary, a good mix of both lighter and softer strokes of the strap, to take her to where she needed to go. She was getting there already, each stroke of the strap no longer causing her to protest but to breathe deeper, her eyes shut tight. He watched her closely. If she did indeed achieve subspace, he'd have to be prepared. Coming down after a subspace session would need particular aftercare.

After the strap came another paddle, a small acrylic one with a wicked bite. He gave her a dozen good swats, all over her tender backside. She was bright red now, a raspberry color, but he'd carefully warmed her up and massaged her, so that he wouldn't hurt her, but rather give her a thorough spanking she'd feel for days and days. He put the acrylic paddle away and came back to her. He lifted his hand and delivered a good, stinging slap of his palm. She shifted and he plunged a finger into her.

He chuckled. "Just what I expected. My good girl is wet again for Daddy. Such a good girl." He pumped his fingers, then removed them, lifting his hand and delivering another sharp swat. She squealed, and he kept going, one swat after another, reveling in the connection of skin-to-skin contact. He loved the power and control the implements gave him, but nothing could compare to the erotic intimacy of a hand spanking, her skin flaming hot to the touch.

He lost track of time. Her eyes were closed and she was breathing heavily, in a stupor-like state, as he spanked on and on. If she trusted him more, he'd have been able to take her to subspace, and she was almost there, already her breathing steady and low. But he didn't want to freak her out. Not now. And shit, he couldn't take one more second of waiting to take her.

He stopped, stroking his finger along her slit, wet with arousal.

"How does that feel, honey?"

"So good, Daddy. So, so good," she said, her words slurred and drunken.

He bent and kissed along her hot, reddened, no doubt aching bottom, then nipped her skin. She gasped as his tongue flicked along the bite-mark before he dipped lower and stroked his tongue along her slit. She moaned out loud. He continued to kiss, and bite, alternating grazing his teeth along her skin and then his tongue, as she moaned and squirmed. Finally, he released the binds fastening her ankles and wrists. But she didn't move. *Was she in sub-space?*

When he walked to where her head lay on the bench, she was grinning.

"How are you doing, baby?" he asked, running a hand along her scalp and squeezing her neck.

"Good, Daddy. Oh, so, *so* good," she repeated.

Perfect.

"Come here, baby," he said softly, placing his hands under her arms and lifting her straight up off the bench. Her head fell to his shoulder as he held her tightly, letting her feel his strength and power. It felt so good to be wanted like this. It was everything he'd yearned for with her. God, he'd do whatever it fucking took to keep her here like this.

He kicked open the door and stalked to his bedroom, giving one last glance at the locked office before he left. He would make love to her. He would make her climax again, and again, and again. He would give her all that she needed from him.

Shit was going down, and how the next few weeks would play out would be telling. She'd need to hold on then. He'd fulfill every fantasy and leave her submitted to him, pining for him, his little Allie-girl's submissive needs met in spades.

Tonight, like every night, she belonged to him.

Chapter 9

A lice lay in Slay's bed savoring the aches she felt all over her body. Her ass was bruised in the most delicious way, her arm muscles had the satisfying stiffness that came from being restrained, her legs felt like jelly from being positioned and repositioned all night long, and she was pretty sure that she had never come so hard or so often in her life. Four times, had it been? Five? *Meh.* Who could count? She'd been in a blissful haze from nearly the first moment Slay had applied the paddle to her backside.

"Six." The deep rasp of Slay's voice had her turning her head on the pillow, her eyes blearily searching through the murky pre-dawn darkness to find him propped on one elbow, staring down at her. Where the heck did he get the energy?

"Hmm?" she mumbled. Honest to God, her lips couldn't even form words.

"That, just a minute ago, was number six," he repeated, as though he could read her mind. His tone was a tiny bit smug, but his eyes devoured the sight of her, spread naked and sated on his bed, with unwavering intensity. He reached out one enormous hand and trailed his blunt, callused finger down the column of her throat, across her collarbone, then down the valley between her breasts. The rough skin of his hand sent streaks of fire zinging up to her brain and down to her pussy, her body so attuned to him, so damn *primed* for him, that she was already arching up to his touch.

It had been like this all night. After the spanking of a lifetime, after getting as close to subspace as she had ever been, Slay had turned to her again and again, alternately fucking her and making love to her. Every time she'd fallen into an exhausted stupor, confident that her body had reached its limit, he'd touch her gently, or just say her name in his soft, gravelly voice, and she'd find that she hadn't come close to reaching her limit yet. It had been frenzied and soul-shattering and amazing. *Her man* had been amazing.

Now, his wicked hand trailed lower, and his palm splayed over her fluttering belly.

"My baby is such a good girl," he approved in a whisper. "She's always ready for what her daddy wants to give her, isn't she, baby?"

His hand was so big that while his thumb brushed her belly button, his baby finger was hovering just above her clit, tantalizingly close.

Despite the exhausted euphoria that had turned her limbs to jelly, she wanted Slay's approval… and fuck but she wanted that finger.

She licked her lips. "Yes, Daddy," she whispered.

He smiled, his teeth bright in the darkness, and his hand moved lower to play with her, his knowing fingers applying just the right amount of pressure to her already sensitized flesh. *Oh, yeah.*

"If Daddy wants to play with her, my baby is ready," he continued.

Alice struggled to focus on his words. He had phrased it as

established fact, not a question, but still she replied. "Yes, Daddy."

He made a rough, approving noise and the movements of his finger became more deliberate, a second and third digit sliding through her wetness to curve inside of her. Oh, God. *Again.* It was building *again.*

"And if Daddy wants to use his mouth on her," he began, leaning forward, until his head was positioned above her breast, then taking one aching nipple in his mouth to tongue it lightly. "My baby is eager." His breath fanned over the wet peak that he'd licked, bit, and suckled throughout the night, until it no doubt glowed a neon raspberry. That whisper of cool air was enough to make her moan.

"*Oh, Daddy,*" she cried as she arched toward him.

"Fuck," he muttered, burying his face in her neck and suckling on the tender flesh there, in exactly the spot that drove her crazy, while his fingers dipped inside her.

How could she be this close, this fast?

"But Allie-girl, what happens if Daddy thinks you've had enough?" he whispered.

Her brain was so clouded by arousal that his words barely registered. But then he removed his hand from her pussy, rolled himself slightly away from her straining, eager body.

"Alice, what happens if Daddy thinks you need some rest right now? What if Daddy thinks his girl needs to sleep?"

She couldn't help the whimper that escaped her.

Oh, heck no! Now? Now, when she was right on the edge?

She reached out one hand to touch him, to run her hand along the hot length of his cock, which was rock hard.

He hissed sharply and grabbed her wrist. "No," he said severely, restraining her hand. "I asked you a question. What do you do if Daddy doesn't give you what you need or want right away, whether it's because he doesn't think you've earned it, or because he doesn't think it's what's best for you, or because he's trying to keep you safe. What does my baby do then?"

Alice blinked, her eyes trying to focus on his face through the murky light and the fog of desire that enveloped her mind. Somehow this conversation felt more emotionally charged than their past conversations about rules and behavior, like he was trying to convey an important message. She struggled to put her brain back together enough to focus.

What would she do if he didn't give her what she needed?

The first thought that came to her was, *Then I'll do it myself,* but she immediately rejected it. At some point over the last week, the idea of handling things on her own, whether it was kitchen faucets or orgasms, no longer gave her the same sense of satisfaction that it once had.

"I wait for you?" She blurted the words out, but haltingly.

"Are you asking me, or telling me?" he demanded, amused.

"I wait for you," she said, more firmly now. "I wait for Daddy to take care of me." The words felt true and right, but one dim corner of her brain, maybe the last remnants of the self-sufficient but incredibly lonely woman she no longer wanted to be, rose up in feeble protest. *My God, what have you just said?*

"That's right," he agreed. "Because Daddy will always take care of you. Things might not happen when and how you *expect* them, Allie-girl, or even the way you think you *want* them, but you can wait for me and know that I'll take care of you. You get me?"

She swallowed. "Yeah, Daddy."

"Good girl," he told her. And then his fingers moved back between her legs, while he rolled his muscled torso over hers. His lips gently parted hers and he licked into her mouth, his tongue thrusting in a rhythm that mimicked the way his fingers pumped into her below.

"You're ready for me," he growled, and though she was already well aware of that fact, the threads of surprise and excitement in his tone made her smile. She placed her hand on his cheek and watched his expression—jaw hard, eyes burning— as he levered himself over her and entered her slowly.

She was so swollen, her flesh so achingly sensitive after the long night, that the firm pressure made her gasp. It was pleasure and pain in just the right combination, and a burn that sated her in the best possible way. He understood, the way he seemed to know everything, just the way she needed him to move, and he rocked over her in slow, nudging thrusts, his pelvis rolling against her clit with just the right amount of friction.

It seemed to go on forever, the pleasure building in waves, and the soft, guttural sounds of arousal, his and hers, filling the room. It was beautiful. It was perfect. And she felt something within her shift on a fundamental level.

The sky got lighter and lighter, until she could clearly see his beautiful, golden brown eyes fixed on her face.

"Come for me, Allie," he told her, his voice sounding almost drunk and as lost to sensation as she was, but his control still firmly in place. And she didn't hesitate. She grabbed onto him tightly with all the strength she could muster, and gave herself over to her daddy.

Three hours later, Alice was looking back on that transcendental lovemaking and wondering if she'd lost her mind. Everything had been so wonderful, and then it had all gone so wrong.

After a record *seventh* orgasm, she'd fallen into a blissful sleep, not through choice so much as sheer exhaustion. But that nap had seemingly lasted all of five minutes before Slay had nudged her shoulder absentmindedly and muttered a gruff, "You said you wanted to be home when Charlie woke up." Slay had been sitting up in bed at the time, his eyes and attention focused on his phone, his thumbs flying over the keys as he sent a text message.

and in that one, moment, all the certainty and *rightness* she'd felt during the night had completely fled, and every doubt and worry had come back with a vengeance. She'd gotten up and dressed herself in the clothes she'd worn yesterday, then let Slay lead her out into the cold morning and help her into his truck for the short but silent ride home.

You're tired, that's all, she told herself firmly. *Thoroughly, gloriously exhausted, and being overly sensitive.* Of course every day wouldn't be like last night! But she'd be lying if she didn't admit to herself that she was hoping the closeness they'd shared would extend a little further, that he would let her in and share some of the secrets he obviously carried. When would he trust her?

Slay smoothly backed his enormous truck into a parking space a block away from Alice's rental house, killed the engine, and reached over to unbuckle her belt.

"There you go, baby," he said distractedly.

It struck her suddenly how expected and routine this had become—the unbuckling of her belt, the sweet "baby" in his gruff voice—even after such a short time. *Too short a time.* It was tempting to think she knew him, but he'd never fully let her in. Had she leapt into this too fast?

At the thought, tension tightened her muscles and anxiety gripped her belly, but she forced herself to smile her thanks anyway. Not that Slay seemed to notice her tension. He opened his door and came around to open hers, but he'd taken his phone from his pocket again and only briefly looked up when she stepped down.

He took her chilly hand firmly in his warm one, and slid the phone back in his pocket as they strolled down the sidewalk. He didn't say a word, and for the life of her, she couldn't think of anything to say either. *Thank you for the incredible night last night!* seemed inadequate. *What the hell is happening?* seemed reactionary. And admitting her doubts and fears the way she knew she probably should seemed impossible when he was so silent and distracted.

The street was mostly quiet at this hour on a blustery December Saturday, and down the street, the neighbor's Christmas decorations blinked cheerily in the early morning light. Alice realized with an uncomfortable rush of guilt that she'd been so consumed with other things in her life—okay, fine, mostly *Slay*—that Christmas was just over a week away and she still had a ton of shopping to do. She debated asking Slay if he wanted to come Christmas shopping, since she knew he almost always had Saturdays off from *Inked* and he wouldn't have to be at The Club until much later. But then she heard the phone buzzing in his pocket once more, and Slay dropped her hand to retrieve it.

She sighed and struggled to keep annoyance from taking root in her brain. Maybe Nora could stay for a few more hours, and Alice could head downtown, knock out her whole list at once. Looked like she'd be on her own once again.

When they were halfway up the path to her door, Slay halted her with a firm hand on her wrist. He glanced down at his phone screen once more—she felt the unreasonable urge to take the phone and throw it against the sidewalk, just to see it crack—and then slid it back into his pocket.

"We need to go over some things, Allie," Slay told her.

"Okay," she said, proud of how calm and controlled she sounded.

"First, remind me who makes the rules," he demanded, his thumb stroking across the back of her hand in a way that both soothed and focused her.

Rules are exactly what you need right now, she reminded herself. If for no other reason than that rules were one of the ways a dom showed he cared.

"You do," she said.

His eyes flared at her admission, lit with some emotion that was both possessive and proud. "That's right, I do, because I'm your daddy, and you trust me to do what's best for you and Charlie."

She gave a short nod.

"Even when you'd rather not," he pressed. "Even when it's not fun."

Alice narrowed her eyes. "O-okay." *Mostly. Usually.*

"You're going to stay home today," he told her. "Rest, make cookies, do whatever you want, but stay inside the house with Charlie all day."

His brown eyes locked on hers in a way that said his decision was not negotiable—a look Alice was very familiar with. Lord knew she'd seen it often enough in the past few days, every time he'd made an unreasonable demand or failed to tell her the truth.

She drew in a long breath and tried to calm down.

When she'd decided to trust Slay last night, she'd thought she'd finally broken through the helpless anger she'd felt at his high-handedness, gotten herself to a submissive, accepting place. Now she realized she'd only pushed it aside temporarily. It had been simmering inside her all along, and now it was threatening to rise up and choke her.

"I'm afraid I can't do that, Slay," she told him. "I have shopping to do for Charlie, so I—"

Slay's eyes had heated the moment she'd said the word "can't." "Do it online," he told her flatly.

"Can you tell me why I should?" Her voice was a demand, but beneath it was a plea. *Tell me why, Daddy.*

He seemed to hesitate, but then his expression firmed. "Because your daddy says so, little girl," he said. "And because you know what will happen if you disobey."

She gritted her teeth and huffed out a breath. *Another one of his tests?* She was getting heartily sick of those.

"Second," Slay continued, but he was interrupted when

Alice's front door flew open and a pajama-clad Charlie came barreling down the stairs.

"Momma!" Charlie cried, his face flushed and his eyes lit up. "Hey, Slay!" he said, with a smile for the man at her side. "Momma, guess what? Grandma and Grandpa came over, and they're going to take us to see the Christmas decorations at the Enchanted Village this morning!"

Alice stared at him. "Grandma and Grandpa are… *here*?" she repeated, looking up at the house as cold horror washed over her.

Charlie nodded. "They brought us donuts!"

Alice's mouth formed a little O, and she looked from Slay to Charlie blankly. Of all the scenarios she could imagine in which her ultra-conservative parents were introduced to Slay, them watching her do the walk of shame into her house after spending the night with her lover—spending a night away from Charlie for literally the first time in his life—was quite possibly the worst.

Shit.

She ran a hand over her tunic sweater, hoping to smooth out some of the wrinkles, but to no avail. She glanced at Slay, to see *completely inappropriate* amusement dancing in his eyes. So, no help from that quarter, either.

With a sigh, she let Charlie grab her hand and tow her up the front steps.

He let go of her hand once they reached the kitchen, and ran ahead to climb up on a stool at the island, snagging himself a donut from the plain white box in front of him. Alice trudged slowly behind, a prisoner heading to the gallows, and not even the promise of donuts could lighten her mood.

She immediately noticed that her parents had made them-selves at home in her kitchen. Her father was sitting on a stool next to Charlie, with one of her red-and-white-patterned coffee mugs steaming in front of him, while her mother stood with her hip resting against the sink. Both of them watched her come in, and she felt exactly like she had seven years ago in *their* kitchen, when she'd had to confess that she'd *sinned* and gotten herself in trouble.

"Uh, hey," she greeted them, feeling Slay stop behind her. He was standing far too close for polite company—she could feel the heat of all six-foot-whatever-inches of him pressing against her back. She tried to ignore him, hoping her parents would also. No such luck.

"Wow, donuts!" she said lamely when neither of her parents returned her greeting.

"From Anna's," her mother said mechanically, her eyes on Slay. "I know they're your favorite."

Alice knew exactly what her parents were seeing when they looked at her man—the bulk, the muscle, the shaved head, the piercings, the tattoos that peeked out from the crewneck and pushed-up forearms of his sweatshirt. Knowing her parents, they'd made an instantaneous decision about Slay, putting him in the category of Criminal and Unsavory Type. They wouldn't see the affection and kindness in his eyes, the way he took care of her, the way he held down multiple jobs, the way he protected everyone he met, all the sweet ways he had connected with Charlie over the past few months—riding kiddie rides at the school fair, debating favorite desserts when Charlie visited her at *Cara*, having deep conversations about X-men. And she didn't know how to *make* them see that. She'd never been able to make them see beyond their prejudices in the past.

So she sighed and focused on donuts.

"They are my favorite," Alice nodded. She cleared her throat. "Let me grab some plates."

Slay grabbed the back of her sweater at the waist and held her in place. "Baby," he said softly, "aren't you going to introduce me?"

She saw her father's face harden at the word *baby*, and felt her own face heat to the approximate temperature of a nuclear reactor.

"Oh. Yeah," she said. "Right. Uh, Mom and Dad, this is, um, A-alexander Slater. Slay, this is my Mom and Dad, Tom and Denise Cavanaugh."

"Call me Alex." Slay stepped forward and held out his hand in friendly greeting to her father, who visibly hesitated before taking it.

Shit shit shit.

"Well," her mother sniffed. "I guess we see now why she hasn't been returning Gary's calls, don't we, Tom?"

Her father, who was locked in a silent staring contest with Slay, didn't reply.

"Mom," Alice began in her placating voice, but her mother overrode her.

"Gary said he's texted you dozens of times, called you twice that much. He said you never even bothered to reply!" she accused, one hand on her hip.

"I was hoping he'd get the hint," Alice mumbled.

This drew Slay's attention to her. "Levitz? He's called you dozens of times?" he demanded.

Alice shrugged. "Well, yeah, but I obviously haven't called him back," Alice said, gesturing toward her mother, who had just hassled her over that very fact.

"Not the point," Slay said, an angry spark in his eye. "What did I tell you, Allie? *If he so much as text messages you, I wanna know.* What part of that was unclear?"

Alice swallowed and felt her face flame impossibly hotter. Yeah, okay, she vaguely remembered that he'd said that, but God! Her parents were right here. Could he tone it down a little? Her dad's jaw was twitching, and her mom's eyes had narrowed.

"Right, okay," she agreed, giving him a pointed look and hoping he would drop it. "Sorry about that."

Slay took a deep breath and tried to compose himself, though she knew she'd be hearing about this... and *feeling* it... later.

"Slay, are you coming with us?" Charlie asked. Alice shifted her eyes to her baby, and found his face obscured by powdered sugar and blueberry filling, his earnest blue eyes watching Slay.

"No, bud, not today," Slay told him, and his little face fell. "I have a lot of stuff to do. And, actually, I think your mom has stuff to do today also, and needs to stay home." Slay turned to pierce her with a hard look. "Isn't that right, Allie?"

Alice blinked back at him. He was going to make them miss the Enchanted Village? He was going to enforce his stay-at-home edict, even when it meant disappointing her parents and Charlie? What was his problem? Was he just trying to prove a point?

She couldn't understand him at all right now, and it scared her. How did everything that seemed as easy as breathing a few hours ago seem so impossible right now?

He wanted her to yield, she knew it. And she knew that maybe, *maybe*, that was her duty as his sub. But… he was supposed to consider *her* needs, too. To factor in what was best for her, and for Charlie. How could he insist on her staying home when her parents were already *here*, when Charlie was so excited?

"Is that true, Alice?" her father demanded. "What do you have to do today?"

"I, uh—" she stammered, staring at Slay and hoping for a reprieve. None came. "I have online shopping to do," she said bitterly.

Slay nodded once, approving, but Alice didn't feel the sense of peace and calm she usually felt when she submitted, when she pleased him. She felt… wronged. And really, really pissed off.

Her eyes narrowed and she opened her mouth to ask to have a word with him in private, when he looked around, seeming to notice something for the first time.

"Where's Nora?" Slay asked.

"Oh, she left," Charlie told him. "When Grandma and Grandpa got here, they told her she could go home. She said she had some things to do anyway, and she'd talk to Momma later."

Sudden tension came over Slay's frame.

"Shi—uh, shoot," he said, with an apologetic look at Charlie. "I need to make a phone call. Be back," he told Alice.

Alice nodded woodenly.

The second he'd stepped out the front door, Alice's mother turned to Charlie. "Charlie, honey, why don't you take your donut in the other room and watch some cartoons?"

"Really?" he said, looking back and forth from his mother to his grandmother.

Alice nodded. She knew she wasn't going to be able to get out of this conversation, so she might as well get Charlie away from it. "But eat over the plate!" she called, as Charlie ran off.

Before her mother could say a word, Alice crossed to the coffee pot and filled herself a mug. She would need fortification for this. She took the first grateful sip.

"Alice. Mary. Cavanaugh," her mother hissed, her eye on the front door, in case Slay should reappear like magic. "Explain yourself."

Her father simply looked at her, cold disapproval in his eyes.

She squirmed… and felt the ache in her bruised posterior protest the movement. The bruises that her man had put there, because she'd wanted him to. Because he cared about her and she… loved him.

Shit.

She really did. She loved him, God help her, even though he made her mad as *hell*. And so, no, she wasn't going to have this conversation, the one where her parents made her feel bad about not being the perfect daughter who followed their rules. Not today. Not *any* day.

She shrugged and returned her mother's gaze directly. "It's pretty self-explanatory, Mom. I'm a twenty-three-year-old woman. Slay is my… boyfriend. We're together."

Her mother inhaled sharply through her nose and pursed her lips.

"I don't like the way he talks to you," her father spat.

Alice controlled her urge to snort. Right, because no one could be high-handed with Alice except *him.*

"Excuse me for a minute," she said. "I need to go and have a word with him."

Her parents clearly weren't pleased, but they said nothing as she left the room and walked to the front door.

Slay hadn't shut the heavy wooden door tightly—it was still open a crack, allowing the chill from outside to blow through the screen door. She took a breath to steady herself, mentally preparing to discuss things calmly and rationally…

And then his voice came through the door.

"Yeah, Diego, that's what I'm saying. Tony says she's not at home, *Cara* isn't open, it's not a school day, I have no fucking clue where she is."

Alice stood, arrested. Diego? *Criminal* Diego? And… were they talking about Nora?

"Fuck. No, everyone else was meeting up with *you*, per your request," Slay said, his voice a harsh whisper. "I kept one guy, Bobby, on the scene to cover both Charlie and Nora. They weren't supposed to split up. When Nora left, Bobby stayed with Charlie."

A pause while Slay ran a hand back and forth over his head and Alice felt her stomach lurch uncomfortably, as though she'd entered another dimension—a dimension where Slay was apparently talking about plans and meetings with one of the bad guys.

"What the fuck do you think?" Slay demanded. "Of course I sent him to find her. Little idiot is going around with pictures of you and Chalo on her fucking phone, begging for trouble, as though falling on your radar wasn't trouble enough." A pause. "Well, now I have a fucking problem, *hermano*, because I'm supposed to be meeting up with you, and who's gonna watch Alice?"

To *watch* her?

Her mind flew back to the night, which seemed forever and

ever ago, when Slay had invited himself into her date with Gary. She'd asked him how he knew where she was, and he'd told her he had a "man" tailing her. She'd assumed he meant someone like him, someone who was a bouncer or an ex-soldier who could keep tabs on her. Now she realized with a sinking feeling that it went much, much deeper than that.

Slay started pacing up and down the front walk. "Who the hell is Victor? I don't want some asshole I've never met over here watching my family," he told Diego.

My family. Alice swallowed. So, not everything had been a lie. The way he felt about her, about Charlie, was real. But beyond that, who *was* this man she'd fallen for? She felt numb.

"No, I know she's not in immediate danger, brother. Not the issue. Would you trust Victor to watch Nora?" he demanded. Then a second later, "Fine. Yeah, okay, I get it. Get Victor's ass over here now. I'll be there in thirty."

He jabbed at the phone screen to disconnect the call, and Alice opened the screen door, pulling the front door shut behind her.

Slay stiffened, but didn't turn around. "How much of that did you hear, Allie?"

"Enough," she said, heartbreak in her voice. "Enough to know that you've been lying to me from the beginning."

He spun around to face her, graceful and imposing. "I have *never* lied to you," he corrected.

She shrugged. "Not telling me the truth is the same as lying, Slay. Who the hell are you, anyway? What are you involved in? How do you know Diego?"

Slay sucked in a sharp breath and cast his eyes from left to right, as though someone were hiding in the bushes watching them. She rolled her eyes.

"We're not having this conversation right now," he told her, and she huffed out a laugh that sounded like a sob.

"Did you ever plan for us to have this conversation at all?" she asked.

He nodded. "When the time was right, yes. Of course. But for now, you need to—"

"Oh, I swear to *God*, Alexander Slater," she said, holding out one hand palm-up. "If you were about to say that I need to *trust you*, you need to back up the bus."

Slay's jaw set and his eyes got hot. In a flash, he was up the steps and in the house, marching her down the hallway to her room.

"What's going on here?" her father demanded as they passed him.

"Allie and I are having a discussion, sir," Slay said, not pausing or slowing down.

"Her name is *Alice*," her father sputtered, but they had already reached her bedroom, and Slay slammed the door shut behind him.

Before he could speak, Alice whirled to face him. "The phone calls, the text messages, the times you couldn't tell me what you were doing... The pictures on Nora's phone. Tell me what's going on, Slay," she pleaded. She gripped his forearm with both of her hands and outright begged in one last-ditch effort, "Please, Daddy, tell me."

He pressed his lips together. "I do security work, you know this," he said.

She waited for him to go on, but he didn't. "You work security at The Club and you helped Blake design the security system. You used to do the same work at Club Black Box. You knew some guys who helped find Nora. None of that, *none*, has anything to do with this," she said, throwing a hand out in exasperation.

"It does and it doesn't," he said, completely unhelpfully. "I do security work for other clients. And I can't say more, Allie. Remember, not *won't*, but *can't*."

She shook her head wildly. "My parents took one look at you and decided you were a criminal, and I was in there *defending you*," she said, gesturing toward the kitchen. "And meanwhile, you're outside having a chat with *Diego,* a guy who was involved in Nora's kidnapping, discussing some *plan* where you're going to work together on something. Explain to me how you have Chalo Salazar's henchman on speed dial!"

His head went back at this. "You think I work for Chalo?" he whispered.

"No!" she denied immediately, instinctively. "No." Whatever she thought, however angry and wronged she felt, she knew he wouldn't do that. "But I don't understand what's happening, either," she admitted.

He remained silent, watching her, and she threw her hands up in frustration.

"You can't keep doing this, Slay! Yes, I'm your babygirl, and yes, I love it. But I'm not a *child*. I don't need you to protect me from the truth. You're asking me to take a huge leap of faith and trust you, but you're not trusting *me*." Her voice broke at the end.

Slay shook his head. "Allie," he began.

A knock on the door made Alice jump.

"Alice! Alice, what is going on in there?" her father demanded.

"Not now, Dad!" she yelled back.

Slay shook his head again. "Baby, this is not the time," he told her, his voice low. "Your parents are here, Charlie is here."

Alice folded her arms across her chest. "Charlie's watching cartoons. And I don't care what my parents think. I submit to you, and I don't need to justify anything to anyone, remember?" she hissed.

His eyes flared. "Oh, I remember, little girl. And I'm glad you do, too," he said, a warning note in his voice now. "Not that you haven't earned yourself one hell of a reminder later, anyway. But people are waiting on me, Alice, and I have to go."

"People more important than I am," she said flatly, refusing to be cowed. Let him spank her. Let him do anything he wanted to her, besides walk out the door with things unresolved between them.

"Hear me, Alice," he said, stepping forward until they were toe to toe, making her look up to keep sight of his eyes as they burned into hers. "There is *nothing* and *no one* more important to me than you."

Alice swallowed. She wanted to believe that. Lord, did she want to believe that she was as important to him as he was to her, but evidence suggested that wasn't the case.

"I will explain everything, I swear, Allie. But right now, I have to go. And when I go, I need to know that you are going to be safe. Someone will be here any minute to keep an eye out, but he can't do that if you're going to be out with your parents or shopping. You need to stay here, with Charlie, to stay safe. Can you do that for me?"

She regarded him silently for a moment, then two. What would happen if she said no? Would he stay? Would he choose to stay with her, keep her safe, rather than going out and doing *whateverthefuck* he was going to do?

But then… did she want to be *that* girl? The kind of submissive who played the brat to get attention? The type of *person* who whined and manipulated? No. That had never been her style.

"Yes," she said. "Fine, I'll stay." But she couldn't help but add in a whisper, "But I'm begging you, Slay, not to go like this. If you don't trust me now, I don't know if we can come back from this."

"We can," he said confidently, his hands reaching out to grab her upper arms and squeeze her to him. "We will. Once I explain everything, once I have time to do that, you'll understand that this was the only way I could play it."

She nodded sullenly, and he leaned his forehead down to touch hers.

"And once you understand, you will know just how badly you have earned the punishment you'll be receiving," he promised, his voice low and harsh.

Her heart skipped a beat, and a pulse of excitement flared in her belly before she ruthlessly quashed it.

He pressed a quick, bruising kiss to her lips before darting out her bedroom door, calling a distracted goodbye to Charlie and her parents as he passed, and leaving her confused, wanting, and majorly pissed off.

"Momma, are you paying attention?" Charlie demanded, glancing up from the movie on his iPad to find her watching her phone, which was still disturbingly free of any communication from Slay, even though he'd left her ten long hours ago.

"Yeah, honey, I'm paying attention," she assured him, running a hand over his silky curls.

Fortunately, she'd seen *How the Grinch Stole Christmas* often enough that Charlie wouldn't catch her in her lie, because she had absolutely *not* been paying close attention. Approximately half of her consciousness was focused on the phone in her hand, willing it to ring, and the other half was thinking up things she needed to say to Slay when he came back.

The list had grown fairly extensive

"But the movie *ended*, Momma," he told her.

Alice squeezed her eyes shut for a moment, then opened them and smiled ruefully at Charlie. "Okay, honey, maybe I was a little bit distracted there at the end," she admitted.

"Is it because Slay isn't here?" Charlie asked.

Ugh. She thought she'd been doing a pretty good job of keeping things from him, but clearly not. Smart kid.

"A little bit, honey. I'm waiting for him to get back," she

admitted. *So I can finally understand what the fuck is happening*, she didn't add.

She'd tried, over the course of the long morning and afternoon, to see his side of things. Once her parents had left, disappointed and annoyed that she hadn't provided any explanation for ruining their plans, she had worked to find her submissive place in all this. But she simply couldn't understand why he hadn't been honest with her from the beginning.

Which meant that likely he didn't *have* a side. He was just plain *wrong*.

And this was no oversight on his part, either. This wasn't him forgetting to tell her about some trivial thing, or not realizing that his actions would have consequences. He did this *on purpose.*

She thought back to their frenzied lovemaking the night before, remembered the way he'd halted in the middle of the action, made her wait, reminded her that things between them might not always happen when and how she wanted them to, but that she should wait for him to take care of her. He *knew* that he was withholding information, and he wanted her to wait for him to reveal it.

But at a certain point, willfully choosing to withhold information, information that in some nebulous way involved her safety and the safety of her boy, was dangerous. There was more at stake here than her trust.

She sighed. Dwelling on this stuff would not solve anything.

"Why don't you take the iPad to my room?" she told Charlie. "I'll make some hot cocoa, and you and I can cuddle up under the covers and watch X-men. Whichever episode you want. And I'll even leave my phone on the dresser," she told him, handing him her phone and drawing a cross over her heart with her finger.

He giggled. "Good deal," he agreed. He bounced off the sofa and down the hall to the bedroom, and Alice headed toward the kitchen.

Until she heard a knock on her front door a minute later.

Slay!

No matter how mad she was, she couldn't contain the joyful leap of her heart, and she couldn't help that the first thought that registered in her mind was not of righteous anger but *Thank God he's home.* She opened the heavy front door, eager for a sight of him…

But it wasn't Slay standing there. It was Douchebag Gary Levitz.

He was smiling warmly at her through the storm door, as though the last time they spoke, he hadn't been marching out of a restaurant while Slay glowered. As though she'd actually returned any of his dozens of calls and texts. She nearly rolled her eyes.

And then he pulled a bouquet of flowers from behind his back. Oh, Lord.

"Hi, Alice," he said. "Your mom said you'd be home today. Can I come in?"

Alice's first instinct was to say no… but then she sighed. He was a jerk, yeah. And no matter how much her parents liked him, she'd learned in her brief time with Slay that she could never, ever be with a guy like Gary. Still, Gary deserved, at the very least, to hear all of that from her, so that he could stop calling her and move on.

"I'll only stay a minute," he promised.

Alice gave him a small smile and relented.

Still, her hand hesitated on the door latch. Slay had specifically told her…

That's only because Slay has some weird jealous fixation. Maybe it would be good for Slay to know that she wouldn't blindly follow his orders, and that trust was a two-way street.

She opened the door and stepped back, allowing Gary to walk inside, then shut the door behind him to block out the chill.

"Gary," she began immediately, "I'm sorry I haven't returned your calls or texts, but I need to tell you… I'm involved with someone else."

Gary turned to face her, and his friendly smile morphed right before her eyes into something sinister.

"Oh, yes, I know. You've been fucking Alexander Slater." He tsked and shook his head sadly. "And thanks to your fuck buddy, my life has gone to hell in the last couple of weeks."

Alice felt her eyes widen and her jaw go slack. What was happening?

"You are such a disappointment to me, Alice," Gary sighed. "Some people just *can't* seem to make decent life choices. I had thought I could help you with that."

Was the man insane? Oh, God, what had she done?

She reached blindly in her pocket for her phone to call for help, but then remembered she'd given it to Charlie. *Charlie*! Oh, God, she prayed he stayed back in her bedroom. Her eyes cut to the front door, and her hand reached for the knob. Did she have time to scream? Would the neighbors hear?

Gary guessed her thoughts immediately and his smile became broader.

"Oh, you don't want to do that, Alice. You really, *really* don't." He still held the bouquet of flowers in one hand, the cheerful yellow daisies now comically out of place. But now he threw the daisies to the floor, sending petals and greenery scattering. From the pocket of his jacket, he extracted a small silver gun and pointed it directly at her.

She gulped, and moved her hand from the knob.

He smiled his friendly smile again, though now she could see that his eyes were… absolutely insane. "See? Aren't you glad I'm here? You're learning to make better choices already."

Then he reached out, grabbed a handful of her hair, and yanked, pushing Alice back against the cold stone of the fireplace.

Pain exploded across her scalp from the way he held her, but she managed to stay silent.

Charlie, Charlie, Charlie, don't come out here! She pleaded with her mind.

"Gary, please," she begged. "I don't know what you want from me."

"I *wanted* to fuck you," he said bluntly. "That's all a bitch like you is good for, you know? But then Alexander Slater started investigating me. Sent my information to the authorities, ruined my fucking reputation, ruined my *life*."

Alice's heart froze at his words. *I wanted to fuck you.* Oh, God, no.

"Please, don't, Gary, please don't," she whimpered.

He laughed, an ugly sound. "Don't what? Fuck you? Take Slater's sloppy seconds? Hell, no. Now I'm just going to fuck you *up*." He paused, as if considering the idea. "Although now that you mention it…"

He pulled her hair even harder, and she bit her lip. His eyes, as they stared down at her, glittered with madness and anger.

"Maybe we'll save that part for when Slater gets here." Then with a smile, he delivered a vicious backhand to her cheek, and Alice cried out.

Chapter 10

S lay pulled onto the intersection of Hawthorne and Main as his phone buzzed. He glanced at the time on the dash and cursed angrily. Thanks to Victor's *fucking timing*, he was running late for the most important phase of the operation to bring down Chalo Salazar, the operation they'd been working on for months. Slay should've been there by now, should have already met up with Diego and the others and gotten into position. But he didn't like leaving Alice and Charlie without a man watching out for them, so he'd stayed longer than he should have, waiting.

Once he had it on good authority Victor was on his way, would be there any minute, he'd forced himself to leave, and tried to focus on the operation despite the niggle of doubt in his mind. Everything was going to be just fine.

Slay picked up his phone and jabbed at the answer button.

"Yeah," he growled, waiting to hear the update from Diego and give his ETA. But instead of Diego's deep voice he heard a softer, higher pitched voice that sounded like a child. It was hard to hear, as the voice was barely speaking above a whisper.

"Mister… Slater? Slay?"

Slay furrowed his brow as he was about to take the right turn onto the Westland Community College campus, where Diego and his crew were waiting. "Charlie?"

"Yes! You have to come," the boy pleaded. "A bad guy came and he hurt Momma! They're in the living room, and I'm in my room. She *screamed*, Slay!"

Fucking *hell*. Rage pulsed in Slay's stomach, ice coursing through his veins as he realized what Charlie was telling him. He gripped the phone so hard he feared it would snap. He was supposed to take a right to get to Diego.

Fuck Salazar. Fuck the sting. He turned his truck around so fast at the intersection, he skidded in front of oncoming traffic, oblivious to the indignant honks of cars yielding to his massive vehicle as he gunned it. He had to get to Alice, and nothing else mattered.

"Did you lock your bedroom door?" Slay demanded.

They'd hurt her. *Someone had hurt her.* What had they done?

Charlie's little voice came back, barely audible. "Yes. I locked the door and called you. I'm hiding in my closet. He doesn't know I'm here, I don't think."

Where the *fuck* was Victor? But he couldn't disconnect from Charlie long enough to find out. He was only minutes away from Alice now.

"Stay on the phone with me," Slay ordered. If the boy was in his closet and his bedroom door was locked, it would be unlikely that anyone would hear from the other side. Still, Slay had to move. A light in front of him turned red, but he powered through it, taking another turn before accelerating. His truck could move when he needed it to, but still, nothing seemed fast enough. Everything seemed too slow, like he was moving through quicksand.

"What did you hear? Did you see anyone?"

"Yes," the boy whispered. "A blond man with a pale face. He looks like the bad guy in the X-men movie, the Senator."

There was only one man Slay knew who was that pale and blond. Fucking *Levitz?*

"What did he do?"

"I… I don't know. He was talking to Momma. I shut the door when he came in because I was watching a movie and I heard him say something. Then I heard him hit her and she screamed. I hope she's okay. I'm scared to go out and see. You have to come."

"Stay *there,*" Slay ordered. "I'm on my way. She will be okay but you do what I say and *don't move.*"

The boy's voice shook. "Okay."

Slay inhaled, trying to calm his pulsating anger. He had to stay calm. If he had Levitz in his hands right now, he'd *kill* him.

"Okay, little man," Slay said, mustering every bit of self control he had, keeping his voice steady with an effort. "I'm almost there."

One block away. If he pulled up too close, Levitz would possibly see him and run, but fortunately her house was adjacent to a small side street. Slay pulled up to the curb, shut his door, and spoke into the phone.

"Charlie? I'm here, buddy. You shut off the phone and stay put. I'm on my way in. You've been brave, my man. Stay brave. I'll be right there."

"I will, Slay," Charlie whispered. The phone went dead as Slay approached the house at a trot. Slay punched a button on his phone to Diego and growled into the phone when Diego picked up.

"Where the hell are you, Slay?"

"I'm at Alice's. Her son called. Levitz is here and the bastard fucking *hit* my woman. Where the *fuck* is Victor? You *said* he was reliable, damn it."

Diego swore. "Slay, we're two minutes out from busting Salazar on campus here, and you're at Alice's? Jesus! I have no idea on Victor. But do you understand that the whole sting is compromised now? We can't do this without you!"

Slay swore into the phone and disconnected. Yeah, he knew he was meant to play a crucial role in bringing down Salazar's drug ring, and he understood that was Diego's priority, but Slay didn't give a shit. Like he'd told Alice earlier, there was nothing and no one more important to him than her.

He approached Alice's back door, which would be easier to bust in than the solid front door. He tried the lock, found it locked tight as he'd ordered her, and in one swift move, reared back before vaulting at the door, the flat of his boot connecting with his full body weight. The thin door and frame splintered under the force as he entered, pulling his gun from his boot and holding it close to his chest. He heard sounds of a struggle and a scream as he moved fast.

Alice and Levitz were in the middle of the living room, Levitz holding her in his sickening grip, her hair pulled taut and head pulled back, as Levitz pointed a silver gun straight at Slay. It was almost as if they'd been waiting for him.

"Perfect," Levitz drawled. "Knew you'd come for her. Wasn't sure how you'd get the word, but I figured one of your henchmen would call you or something."

Slay's hands shook with fury as he watched Levitz with narrowed eyes.

"Her mom knew she was home today," Levitz said. "Told me I'd find her here. Her dad suggested the flowers." Levitz grinned. "The metal was Salazar's suggestion." They stood, the two of them pointing guns at one another.

"Drop your weapon, Levitz," Slay ordered in a low voice, but Levitz had Alice, putting him at a decided advantage.

Levitz cocked a brow. "Excuse me? Considering I'm the one holding the bitch, it seems *you* should be the one dropping your weapon."

A door knob sounded in the hallway.

"Charlie, no!" Alice yelled at the same time Slay yelled, "Stay!"

Levitz' eyes widened. "Ah, you two both seem concerned about the boy. Did it ever occur to you, Alexander *Slater*, that if you hadn't gotten your nose stuck where it didn't belong, I'd have maybe left these two alone? Hmm?"

"And did it ever occur to you, Levitz, that I'd have let you live if you'd left them alone?" Slay growled. Alice screamed as Levitz yanked her head back, his eyes narrowed to slits as he watched Slay, but suddenly, a loud noise sounded like a gunshot in the hallway, and all heads jerked toward the sound. Levitz was holding Alice, but the second he moved, she twisted, elbowing him hard in the ribs. Levitz doubled over, his weapon flying out of his hand and spinning out onto the floor. Slay wasted no time. With one swift move, he dove toward Levitz, yanking him away from Alice. He shoved her to the floor.

"Go for cover!" he shouted as he swung a fist and hit Levitz's jaw. Slay heard the sickening snap of bone, felt the satisfying connection in his hand as Levitz swore and crumpled. Slay yanked him to his feet and swung his fist again, this time hitting him straight in the gut, causing him to wheeze and gasp, just as Slay kneed him. Another sharp blow to the chest landed, his own gun now forgotten, as Slay viciously delivered blow after blow.

"You'll kill him!" Alice said, getting to her knees and holding her hands out to Slay.

"Stay there!" Slay roared, letting loose another kick to Levitz who now lay on the floor, but it was the last blow he delivered. He *could* kill him. He *wanted* to kill him. But she was right. He lifted Levitz by the shirt, and was satisfied to see him slouch without a fight. He grabbed his phone out of his pocket, panting from the exertion, his eyes fixed on Alice.

"Come to Alice's. It's too late to bag Salazar, but Levitz is down."

"It was brilliant," Alice said, as she handed Charlie a steaming mug of hot cocoa. "I never would've thought of it. It's sorta scary how realistic they make those apps sound these days."

"Damn, I need that app myself," Slay said. After Diego sent a man to take Levitz in, Charlie had revealed to them all how he'd used an app on Alice's phone to make it sound like a gunshot in the hallway, to distract "the bad guy." Alice had downloaded an app months ago with realistic gun sounds, and Charlie often entertained himself going "hunting" in the backyard. Who would've thought the kid was smart enough to fake out a real criminal with the thing?

Charlie sat at the table, swinging his feet. It was hours later, after Diego's men had apprehended Levitz and questioned Alice. Slay sat at the table next to Charlie, drained, not having had a chance to even talk to Alice yet. She had no visible injuries, and even Slay had been miraculously unscathed, so he'd allowed her to stay home and avoid the hospital. But he watched her interacting with Charlie as best she could, and he wondered. Where would they go from here? Where did this leave them?

Levitz had been neutralized, Nora was found safe, having gone to work, and thank God Alice and Charlie were now safe. But Slay's removal from the scene had effectively short-circuited the sting operation, costing them months of work and planning. Salazar had slunk away and likely wouldn't emerge now for some time. The sting was not going to happen. Slay could only hope that the threat to Salazar would be enough to thwart his efforts.

Alice was safe. Charlie was safe. And that was what mattered. But he replayed Alice's words from earlier that morning, telling him that if he left, they might never be able to come back from that, and he wondered if *he* and Alice would be okay. Could she forgive him for not keeping her safe?

Alice had seemed as if she were on auto-pilot earlier, shrugging off his touch and answering Diego's man's questions honestly, and he recalled the terror in her voice.

"I don't know what would've happened if Slay didn't get here," she'd whispered. "Anything could've happened. Charlie…" She'd covered her face with her hands but she did not cry. She didn't say much more than that either. Did she blame Slay for leaving?

"Time for bed now," she said to Charlie when his mug was empty. She still didn't meet Slay's eyes, as she ushered Charlie down the hall to his bedroom. And still, Slay sat at the table, as he heard the water going on and off as Charlie brushed his teeth, followed by the murmured sounds of Alice reading him a bedtime story. Darkness settled in the kitchen as he waited for her, not moving, and he grew cold. Why would he move? He had nowhere go to. He had no idea where this left him.

Standing up to stretch, he moved into the living room and sat heavily on her sofa as his phone buzzed. Diego.

He's behind bars, man. Levitz won't touch her again.

Slay nodded at the phone as he typed. *And Salazar?*

Spooked, as expected. Word's been passed down through his organization that we're going to scale back operations for the time being. No more Westland CC. No more P&B. Mindy Freeman's been encouraged to disappear. But don't worry. We'll wait for him to fuck up again and we'll nail him. Might take a few months, but it'll happen.

Slay hoped it would be sooner rather than later. He itched to put the bastard away.

Lost in his own thoughts, he never heard Alice approach until she was standing in front of him. He hated the look in her eyes. She looked… guarded. On edge. Angry, even.

"Slay?"

"Yeah, babe?" he said with a sigh.

"Charlie wants you to tuck him in," she said, and her voice caught at the end as she looked away. She bit her lip, nervously twisting a piece of golden hair in her hand. He stood, leaned in and kissed her forehead.

"Sure thing, baby," he said, walking down the hallway to Charlie and leaving Alice behind him. What would he say to the boy? What if tonight was good-bye? But no, that had to come from Alice, not him.

A dim nightlight in the shape of a lightning bug shone in the wall outlet as he entered the bedroom. Charlie's eyes looked half-lidded, but he smiled as Slay approached the bed and sat on the edge, his heavy frame making the bed sag and creak.

"Slay?" Charlie whispered.

"Yeah, buddy?" Slay asked, folding his hands on his lap.

"Is Momma safe now?" Charlie asked.

"Course she is," Slay growled, more forcefully than he intended. He softened his voice. "She's safe thanks to you, little man."

Charlie smiled. "And you," he said. Slay ruffled his hair. "Will they come back?"

Slay shook his head, his heart twisting in his chest. Poor kid. "Course not, Charlie," he said. "The bad guy's in jail now. And he's not coming back."

Charlie nodded. "Will you stay tonight? Just in case?"

Slay closed his eyes briefly. How could he stay? He opened his eyes to catch Charlie staring at him seriously.

"Not—not for me, Slay," he said, lifting his chin bravely. "I… I'm fine. But… you know, for Momma. Sometimes she gets scared at night and has bad dreams. I've heard her. But… maybe she wouldn't if you were here. Will you stay with her?"

Slay smiled sadly. "If she wants me to, Charlie. If she wants me to, you have my word."

Charlie smiled, closing his eyes and rolling over on his side. "Good then. You'll stay. She doesn't want you to go."

Slay leaned in, tucking the navy blanket over Charlie's shoulder, wishing he was as sure of that. "Sleep tight, little man. Dream of bravery and heroes, and know you're one of them."

Charlie smiled, though his eyes remained shut. Slay got to his feet and went to Alice. How would he explain to her what they'd just talked about? But as he entered the hallway, Alice was standing right there, her eyes brimming with tears. He felt his own eyes widen as he watched her. Was she okay? He took a tentative step toward her, and she fairly leapt into his arms, the ferocity of her grasp taking him by surprise. He lifted her up, and she wrapped her legs around his waist. She buried her face in his neck. Her shoulders shook, and he heard a loud sniffle. He slowly walked away from Charlie's room so Charlie wouldn't hear, holding her against his chest, feeling like it was the most natural thing in the world.

"Baby," he soothed, planting a kiss to the top of her head. "Honey, it's all right. Levitz is gone. You're safe now."

Her voice was hushed, and she hiccupped when she talked to him through her sobs. "I—I'm so sorry, Daddy," she whispered. "I—I didn't believe you. I disobeyed you. I should've listened to you. I should've trusted you. I didn't. I was so bad. How could you ever forgive me?" she wailed.

His heart twisted again as he closed his eyes briefly, sinking down to the sofa with her on his lap.

I'm sorry.

Forgive me.

Daddy.

So it wasn't over then. No. No, not by a long shot, because his girl was willing to work it through. She saw the truth now, she recognized it for what it was, and wanted his forgiveness.

Fucking hell. It wasn't all over. Hell, no.

They'd just begun.

"Baby," he said. "Daddy's glad you're safe. And we can work through this, Allie," he said. "I thought you were done with me, with us. All night, you've looked like you were ready to send me packing."

"I was trying to hold it in!" she wailed. "All of it. How badly I felt. How scared I was. How relieved I was when you came for me. I knew all along that you'd come for me."

"Baby," he whispered, pulling her head down to his chest in a fierce hug. "God, baby. What a night you've had."

She sniffled. "He could've killed me and hurt my boy," she wailed. "But you saved us. And I heard Charlie asking if you'd stay. Will you stay… Daddy?"

"Of course, baby," he crooned. He held her quietly in the darkened room, until her sobs quieted and she seemed to visibly lighten from having cried it all out.

"Forgive me, Daddy?" she whispered.

He inhaled, then exhaled slowly. She'd been hurt tonight, but his babygirl needed her daddy now. She didn't *just* need soothing words and a shoulder to cry on, she needed the accountability and discipline that a daddy would provide. And hell if he wasn't willing and able to give it to her.

"Of course I forgive you," he said, trailing his hands through her golden hair, smoothing it back from her forehead. "But I think something has to happen so that you can forgive yourself. Don't you agree, honey?" He ran his finger along her cheekbones, wiping away the tears.

She lifted her head off his chest and looked at him bravely. "Yes," she whispered. "I… disobeyed you," she said, her eyes lowered as she looked at her hands and bit her lip. "Put myself in danger. Didn't trust you. And I want this behind us. Will you help me with that, Daddy?"

He nodded slowly. Yes. He *had* forgiven her. Now he'd give her what she needed so that she could forgive herself. "You know I will, Allie. You're my babygirl. And Daddies always give their babygirls what they need." He took a deep breath as he made his decision. "Do you trust me to do what's right for you?" he asked.

She nodded, lifting her face to his. Brave girl. His strong, courageous girl. He reached his hand to her and tucked a stray piece of hair behind her ear, speaking softly but firmly. She needed to listen, and obey. "Tonight, I'm going to tuck you into bed. I'm going to hold you until you fall asleep, and I'll be here when you wake up in the morning. I'm not going home tonight. And tomorrow? We'll go to my place and do what we need to."

She closed her eyes briefly but when she opened them she looked at him fearlessly. She nodded. "Yes, Daddy. And Slay?"

"Yes, baby?"

"I love you. I know that now. I do. I love you."

He pulled her head to his mouth and kissed her fiercely.

"And I love you, baby. Let's get you ready for bed."

He hoisted her in his capable arms as she sank her head on his chest. She was so tired; he could feel the dead weight in his arms as he carried her. Lowering her onto her bed, he left her there while he fetched a nightie from the top drawer in her dresser. He slipped off her clothing, helped her get dressed, then sent her to the bathroom to ready herself for bed with a teasing swat. She giggled and tried to tease him by straddling his hips and trying to make out. His baby was coming back, slowly but surely.

He kissed her, then lifted her up and another sound swat had her hopping. He wasn't going to let her derail them. There would be time for much more later. Tomorrow, he'd take her across his lap and cleanse her of all that had transpired. Tonight, she needed sleep. She needed her daddy.

Chapter 11

Alice sat in the front seat of Slay's truck, her hands wrapped around a steaming paper coffee cup as they drove down the streets of Slay's neighborhood in the late afternoon sunlight. But although Slay had made a point to buy her favorite kind, and the delicious cinnamon scent of it curled appealingly around her, she couldn't relax enough to take a single sip. Her stomach was a hard knot of worry, her chest tight with tension.

She pushed her lips together nervously, darting a glance at the man beside her. Slay's hands were on the wheel, his eyes focused on the road, but she could tell by the way his jaw was locked, by the slight stiffness in his posture, that he wasn't relaxed either. Not at all.

They'd talked things over last night, and they'd finally said they loved each other—a moment so perfect and beautiful that she'd already replayed it in her mind a hundred times today—but somehow things still felt unresolved between them. She couldn't tell if her anxiety came from feeling like he was still angry at her, or if she was simply angry at *herself*. The severity of her mistake yesterday brought tears to her eyes, and she knew she'd never be able to move past it until she knew for sure that he *truly* forgave her. That couldn't happen until she'd paid the price for disobeying him.

The thought made her pause for a second. Was that weird? That she required *his* forgiveness first? And as quickly as the thought came, she dismissed it. She was beyond giving a shit what was *weird* or *not weird*. She and Slay had a system that worked for them, and that was all she cared about. Other people's opinions didn't matter to her in the slightest anymore. She was a babygirl who needed absolution from her daddy.

And her newfound I-don't-give-a-shit attitude had definitely made it a lot easier to bring Slay to her parents' house this afternoon. She'd called her mom that morning, at Slay's suggestion, just to clear the air. Yesterday had marked the first time in her adult life that she'd stood up to them, and she'd wondered whether they'd hold a grudge. But Slay had reminded her gently that if she wanted a relationship with them on her terms, she had to make the first step, and not allow them to control her.

She'd been stunned to find that her parents were not just willing but *eager* to mend fences. They invited Alice, Charlie, and Slay to spend the afternoon. After consulting Slay, Alice had agreed to a short visit, but she'd been dreading it all morning. The weight of her impending punishment still lay on her shoulders, and she'd been unsure whether her parents would be capable of remaining civil all afternoon.

She'd been unprepared for the warm reception they'd received.

Her father had surprised her by offering his hand to Slay the moment they'd stepped inside the house, and then absolutely *shocked* her by apologizing for intruding yesterday without consulting her first. Alice had gaped at Slay, wide-eyed, while her father wrapped her in a tight embrace. Slay had only shrugged and smiled.

Alice's mother had taken Charlie to the kitchen to prepare

some snacks. Since Denise Cavanaugh's need to feed the people she loved put Tony Angelico's to shame, this had turned out to be enough food to feed an army.

Meanwhile, her father had taken Alice and Slay to the family room, where *of course* the Patriots game was on, and ushered Slay into his own favorite recliner.

"Ah, not this again. Why do they keep handing off to Bleeker?" Slay had demanded, his eyes fixed on the screen before he'd even sat down. "Every game, it's the same damn thing."

Her father's eyes had lit up at this evidence of a Pats fan who knew what he was talking about.

"No shit," he had agreed. "I keep telling Denise, we pay enough for Gladstone's arm, we have enough receivers, the boy needs to be throwing."

"When Conrad was the QB, this wasn't an issue," Slay had griped. "Back when I was in the Marines, we caught a game out in San Diego…"

"You served?" her father had asked, looking at Slay with new respect.

"Yes, sir," Slay had confirmed, and her father had launched into a discussion of his own short stint in the Army just after high school.

And just like that, "Alex-the-tattooed-criminal-type" was now her father's new BFF, and had a standing offer to come over and watch the game on her father's big-screen TV anytime.

The change of heart had been baffling. Like, *Twilight-Zone* baffling. What happened to wanting a nice, white-collar, church-going man for her? But then she'd gone into the kitchen to help Charlie and her mom with the food, and had seen this morning's *Herald* laid out on the kitchen table.

Financial Analyst Tied to Drug Cartel the headline blared, above two enormous pictures of Gary Levitz—one showing him smiling and smarmy in better days, and the other showing him wild-eyed and disreputable-looking at his indictment hearing, sporting an enormous bruise on his jaw and wearing jail-issued scrubs.

Ah, mystery solved.

Her mother had glanced over and noticed Alice looking at the paper. She'd wet her lips nervously and sent Charlie out with the first batch of snacks before saying, "Alice, I need to apologize."

Alice had mentally rolled her eyes. Thanks to Slay and the men he worked with, her name had been kept out of the newspapers, and Alice and Slay had agreed that telling her parents about Gary's attack wouldn't serve any purpose, so her mother had no idea just how *much* she had to apologize for. But Alice appreciated the effort.

They'd hugged, and her mom had cried a little. "I only want you and Charlie to be safe and happy, Alice," she'd said.

"Then please believe me when I tell you that dating Slay is the best way to ensure that both of those things are true, Mom," Alice had told her.

Charlie had returned for more snacks, her mother had quickly dried her eyes and fixed her grandson with a bright smile, and the moment had passed, but it had given Alice hope.

When her parents had asked them to stay and watch the rest of the game, Slay had immediately agreed, and Alice was glad he had. Still, while the afternoon had helped bring their family closer together than ever, it had left her situation with Slay completely unresolved.

Slay had been all-in with her from the beginning, and she'd done nothing but doubt and question him, even putting Charlie's life in jeopardy with her mistrust and disobedience. Oh, sure, she'd had her reasons, but none of them seemed very compelling right now. She remembered Slay saying that once he'd explained everything, she'd understand, and boy was he right.

He'd told her to trust her man, but when the circumstances were most dire, she hadn't.

How could she show him that she was sorry, that she was committed to building a life with him as her daddy? Did he really even want her to anymore?

She couldn't help but notice that Slay wasn't glancing at her as much as he usually did, and that he hadn't smiled at her all day. Was he having second thoughts about their relationship? Had he realized that she was just too much work?

As the game wore on, the multitude of snacks were consumed, and high-fives were exchanged between the men (and the boy), Alice had felt her emotions ratcheting up higher and higher. And that was even *before* her mother had suggested letting Charlie stay overnight!

Charlie slept over at his grandparents' house from time to time, but with all the trauma and drama of the day before, Alice was none too eager to have her boy out of her sight for even a minute. She needed the reassurance of being able to hug him, to run her hand through his silky blond curls, to remind herself that he was all right.

But before Alice could shake her head or form a word protest, Slay had leaned over, placed a firm hand on her knee, and said, "I think that would be a great idea, don't you, Allie?" To her parents, he'd given a friendly smile and explained, "Alice and I do have a few things we should take care of today," as though they were planning to run errands or clean out the kitchen junk drawer. Then he'd turned to her, his gorgeous eyes half-lidded and smoldering, and without conscious thought, Alice's thighs had clenched with nervous anticipation.

They'd said their goodbyes and gotten enthusiastic hugs from Charlie before he ran off to bake Christmas cookies with his grandmother, then departed. But when Slay had buckled her into the passenger's seat, he'd sat back, looking at her and frowning thoughtfully.

"You're gonna need coffee," he'd pronounced.

Alice, who had been expecting a much grimmer pronounce-

ment involving misbehavior and its consequences, had been star-
tled. "What?"

"My girl needs coffee," he'd elaborated. "The pumpkin spice
shit you get."

Alice had blinked. That was so thoughtful of him, but…
"No, thank you. I…"

"Can't sleep at night if you drink coffee in the afternoon?"
he'd asked dryly, his caramel eyes burning into hers. "Oh, I
know."

Those three simple words spoken in his deep, rumbling voice
had made her shiver. And then he'd fallen quiet. He'd gotten her
the coffee, and they'd driven the last twenty minutes in fraught
silence.

What was he thinking? What would he do to her? What
could she say to make everything better?

He slid the truck easily into a parking space near his building
and reached over to unfasten her seatbelt.

"I bought the coffee so you could *drink* it, Allie," he said. "Not
stare at it."

She nodded and brought the cup to her lips obediently.

He shook his head and regarded her with something that
looked almost like amusement, as impossible as that seemed.

He came around to open her door and help her out, then
guided her to his building with his hand wrapped possessively
around the back of her neck.

As he opened the door to the building, a nearby apartment
door opened, and a pair of bright blue eyes peeked out.

"Alexander Slater! I thought that might be you! When are
you gonna buy me a drink?"

Slay stopped short, and his face morphed into a bright smile
as the door opened wider and an older woman whose curly grey
hair barely reached Slay's breastbone peeped out.

"Hey, Betty," he said.

"Don't you 'hey, Betty' me, young man," Betty scolded with

twinkling eyes. "Did you think I'd forget that we had a date?" Betty's eyes met Alice's and the older woman smiled. "Oh, I see! You've found a sweet young thing to feed you cookies and you don't need me anymore!"

Alice's eyes widened. Feed him cookies? Young man? *Slay?*

Beside her, Slay chuckled. "Now, Betty, you know you'll always be my first love, but you're way out of my league! This is my girl, Alice."

His girl. It soothed something inside her to know that, angry as he was, that hadn't changed.

"Pleased to meet you," Alice said, holding out her hand.

Betty grasped her hand in a surprisingly tight grip and leaned forward to whisper, "Tell me, has he taken *you* to The Club for a drink?"

Alice coughed and stared at Slay with wide eyes. How the heck did this lady know about The Club?

Slay pressed his lips together and he shook his head, fighting laughter. Before Alice could speak, Betty waved a hand through the air dismissively. "Never mind. One of these days, we'll all go together. I haven't been to a club since my Herman passed away," Betty said. "Lord rest his soul. But this one reminds me of my Herman." She nodded fondly at Slay.

Alice was flooded with sympathy. "Did he pass away recently?"

"Lord, no. Forty years this July. And I haven't been to a disco since 1974… but a club is a club, isn't it?" she asked eagerly. "Music, drinks, women wearing dresses shorter than they should?"

"Well… I suppose that's true," Alice found herself agreeing, loving the feeling when Slay's big hand squeezed her neck in approval.

"You might find it a bit tame for you, honestly," Slay told Betty with a straight face. "But we'll take you."

He clapped a hand over his chest as if swearing an oath.

making Betty's face light up. Alice's heart melted into a pile of goo.

"You've got yourself a good one, girl," Betty told Alice with a smile. "Don't let him go."

"No, ma'am," Alice replied instantly, her eyes on Slay's. "I promise, I never will."

Slay's face changed in an instant and his veneer of civility fell away. He was no longer joking, easygoing Alex, nor the polite but distant man he'd been earlier that day, but her daddy, her dominant, and his eyes blazed with possessive fire.

"Excuse us, Betty," Slay said brusquely. He grabbed Alice by the hand and towed her away.

"Yes, *just* like my Herman," she heard Betty sigh before she was out of earshot.

And then, within seconds, Alice was inside Slay's apartment. He kicked the door shut, then turned and pushed her back against it, like a flashback to their first time together, to what had begun in that tiny, chilly room at The Club.

It was so similar… and so completely different.

That night, just a few short weeks ago, she'd been fighting him, fighting *them*. She'd wanted his body, craved his dominance, but hadn't been ready to trust, to truly give up control. To give him her heart.

She was now.

His lips found hers, and their tongues tangled in a rhythm that felt immediately familiar and right, and his hands slid up her hips, over her waist, under her sweater, claiming territory he already knew he owned. His thumbs found the bottom band of her bra, and smoothed back and forth over her ribcage for a moment before he pulled back and stared down at her.

"You ready, Allie?" His eyes smoldered and his voice was husky with desire, but his jaw was set.

Alice swallowed and nodded. Punishment time. She'd been dreading it and craving it all afternoon—the spanking, the confession she needed to make, and the step she knew she needed to take.

Slay stepped back and held out a hand for her. She immediately took it… and let him guide her back to his "office." But when he'd unlocked the door and pushed it open, she darted inside first and put a restraining hand on his chest.

His eyes narrowed.

"I know that I need to be punished. I don't want it, but I need it," she told him softly. "And not just because I let Gary in yesterday, or because of what could have happened if you hadn't saved Charlie and me."

She saw Slay's jaw twitch at the mention of Gary's name, and she hurried on. "I need to be punished because I didn't *just* make a mistake. I deliberately disobeyed you when I let him in," she whispered. Her eyes flooded with tears and she quickly blinked them back. "You were right the other night when you said I didn't want an explanation, I wanted an… an excuse. A reason to guard my heart from you. When I let Gary in, I knew you'd be mad. I wanted you to be. I wanted to see if *that* would be the thing that made you change your mind about me, about *us*."

He inhaled sharply, and she glanced up. His eyes watched her face steadily, but he didn't seem surprised. Rather, it was as though she'd said something he'd suspected but hadn't expected her to admit. She stumbled on.

"I realize now, though," she hesitated, taking a deep breath before plunging ahead. "That I got it all wrong from the beginning, didn't I? You're not going to leave, even if I mess up, are you?"

He shook his head slowly. "You're stuck with me now, Allie-girl. For as long as you want me."

Joy ripped through her, dissolving the ache in her chest and leaving her trembling. "And if I want you forever?"

He smiled and his eyes kindled with unbridled heat. "You're

the first girl who's ever called me Daddy, Allie. I've never been that for anyone else, and I swear to you, I never will. Clothes off. Now."

She sucked in a deep breath. "I was thinking maybe I could maybe wear… *something*."

He cocked an eyebrow and folded his arms across his chest, making the muscles in his arms bunch beneath his sweatshirt. God, she could feel herself getting wet just looking at this man. *Her* man. Her *daddy*.

She spun around and quickly walked to the wall where the tawse, the Wartenberg wheel, and the other tools of his craft hung unused (at least thus far), and grasped the silky black blindfold. She turned back to face him, grasping the fabric so tightly that it wrinkled in her hand.

"This is… I couldn't… I've never been able to handle being blindfolded," she stammered. "I couldn't stand not knowing, not being able to see what came next. But with you?" She reached for his hand and deposited the blindfold in his open palm. "I know that it doesn't matter what comes next, as long as my daddy is taking care of me."

Slay sucked in a deep breath and his nostrils flared, as though his control was being tested. The hand with the blindfold reached out to snag her around the waist and draw her against his hard chest for another deep, mind-melting kiss.

"Baby," he said when he broke away, his voice deeper than she'd ever heard it. "You will not regret this."

She smiled, started to tuck herself more deeply into his chest, but he put his hands on her arms to hold her away, then walked her over to the large, padded bench. He knelt before her and, with careful hands, removed her shoes, her jeans, and her sweater, his fingers barely touching her eager flesh. Then he stood and backed away.

"Kneel for Daddy," he told her, pointing to the bench.

Once she was in position, with her lower legs cushioned by the padded kneelers, Slay came up behind her and slid the blindfold around her eyes, tying it snugly and cutting off her view of the world.

She sucked in a deep breath as panic threatened to overtake her, and forced herself to calm.

"That's my baby," Slay told her. "God, I'm so proud of you. You stay in position, honey."

His words made warmth blossom in her chest. She would hold her position. She'd stay just like this forever if he asked her to.

But of course it wouldn't be that easy.

With a firm hand between her shoulder blade, Slay pushed her torso down onto the bench, his big hand easing her into position until her cheek was resting against the padded leather and her ass was fully on display. Then Slay's hands disappeared.

She'd never felt so completely exposed, so totally vulnerable. *Shit*. Minutes that felt like hours passed in absolute silence as she lay there, and only the harsh sounds of his breathing and the rustle of his clothing as he moved about the room reminded her that she wasn't alone.

Submitting, *trusting*, were always so much easier in theory.

And then he returned, running a large, calloused hand down her back.

"You messed up, Allie," he said, matter-of-factly. "You deliberately disobeyed me. You put yourself and Charlie in danger."

Panic made her voice tremble as she replied. "Yes, Daddy."

No sooner had the words left her mouth, when the sharp crack of his broad palm striking her ass rent the air, making her yelp.

Oh, Jesus. Was it possible that it *hurt* more with the blindfold on? A dozen or more swats followed, the sharp clap of flesh-on-flesh broken only by her whimpers as she tried not to squirm too much. Every stroke of his hand set her rear end on fire, until it was hot and throbbing.

But then the hand paused, rubbing against her gently as though savoring the way her flesh pulsed with heat beneath it.

"Do you know what I would have done, if that asshole had really hurt you, if he'd touched a single hair on Charlie's head?" he demanded, his voice rough with emotion.

Alice swallowed and shook her head against the bench.

"Answer me, Alice," he demanded. He had moved, and his voice was a hot breath against her ear now, sending shivers up her spine.

"No, Daddy," she said aloud.

"Neither do I," he said softly, as though it were wrenched from him, and her heart stuttered. "I've waited for you a long time, Allie. Fucking forever. Since the day I was born. And now that I've found you, I'm not going to lose you, you get me? You will not take chances."

"I get you, Daddy," she whispered, chastened. It had simply never occurred to her, as she wrestled with her own fears and insecurities over the past day, just how frightened big, tough, Alexander Slater had been.

"If you don't get me now, you soon will, Alice," he promised, and she bit her lip.

A second later, a whistle of sound, and then the sting of leather as it hit the top of her thighs made her jump.

"Slay!" she cried. "What *is* that?"

"Stay in position," he told her inexorably. "You hold your position, baby."

Another *thwap!* And another. And another.

Oh, God! She cried out with each stroke now, unable to stop herself from writhing as each one fell. She tried not to tense against the pain, but found it impossible when she couldn't see, when she didn't know when the next blow would be coming. Tears leaked from behind her eyelids to soak the blindfold as the stinging swats rained down.

"You will not take chances. You will not condemn me to a life without you. Do you understand?"

"Yes! Yes, Daddy," she sobbed, nearly as undone by his words as she'd been by the pain. Her tears were flowing freely now.

She heard a dull *thunk* as he dropped the implement he'd been using to the floor, and then Slay's hand was rubbing her ass, soothing the sting, removing her from the bench, lifting her into his arms, and finally, *finally*, removing the cursed blindfold from her eyes.

"Hush, baby," he whispered, as he sank to the floor, cradling her in his arms. "Hush."

"I'm s-so sorry, Slay," she told him, reaching up a hand to his cheek. "Can you forgive me?"

He shook his head. "Allie, honey, I already have. That's how this works. I'm your daddy. I will always love you. I'll always forgive you." He gave her ass a soft squeeze that made her cry out. "And I will always give you what you need, even when what you need is a thorough spanking."

Alice sniffled and nodded. She'd never take for granted how attuned he was to her, how he knew exactly when she needed a long, unyielding spanking, and when she craved comfort. Right now, every fiber of her being cried out for Slay and the peace that only he could provide.

She was cherished.

She was safe.

She was forgiven.

Slay bent his head to bite her bottom lip softly and then, as if he couldn't help it, he kissed the spot he'd bitten… and before she knew what was happening, she'd gone from being cradled in his arms to straddling his lap, rubbing herself along the erection that strained against his jeans.

"Slay?" she gasped, breaking away from the kiss to run her tongue along the corded strength of his neck. "What if I need you to take off your clothes right this second and make love to me?"

His smile was incandescent, and his brown eyes glowed with laughter.

"Anything for my babygirl," he told her. And then proceeded to prove it.

Epilogue

Alice pushed open the front door of The Club and took a grateful gulp of cold night air. She lifted her hair up off her neck and felt the sweat she'd worked up evaporate. Good Lord, the people on the dance floor were maniacs—and that was just the people she'd *come here* with!

She ambled up the short walkway to the street, the better to admire the twinkling Christmas lights that still hung in the trees. They'd likely be taken down next week, around the time Charlie headed back to school after Christmas break, and the neighborhood would lose this little touch of magic. But then again, if things worked out the way she hoped, she wouldn't be around here often enough to miss them.

"You behaving, Allie-girl?"

That deep, gravelly voice, now so familiar, still had her whirling around and clutching her throat.

"Alexander Slater!" she admonished. "You still move *way* too silently for a man your size!"

"That so?" He wrapped his arms around her waist, and dipped his mouth close to whisper in her ear. "You had no complaints about the way I moved earlier today."

His words made a happy shiver dance up her spine and he chuckled. "You turned on already, baby?" he asked.

Arrogant man. "I'm *chilly*," she told him primly, making him laugh again.

"Well, then, I'd better warm you up," he agreed, pulling her against his chest.

She sighed and sank against him.

"I was just thinking I was going to miss this place," she told him. "If I get accepted at the University."

"*When* you get accepted," he corrected. "The lady in the admissions office told you they'd be happy to accept the credits for the classes you took a few years ago."

"Yeah," Alice breathed, almost unable to believe it had been so easy. "They have lots of programs for part-timers, too. I'm excited… but I'll miss it here."

"Yeah… no drunk assholes leering at you when you wear your short leather skirt, no being propositioned to participate in demonstrations with strangers." His voice hardened. "Such a shame."

Alice giggled and buried her smile in his neck. "I *meant* the fun, the acceptance, Blake's dry humor…"

Slay snorted and ran his hand up her back to slide down her long, blonde hair. "Blake's humor. The man has barely smiled in three months."

Alice grimaced. "Okay, true. This hasn't been his happiest hour. Is it true that his wife…

"I'm not gonna talk about it, baby, and I'm not gonna specu-late. He's going through one of the hardest things any *man* ever has to go through, let alone a *dominant* like Blake. When he's ready to tell everyone what's happening, he will."

Alice blew out a breath and nodded. It was hard not to worry when you saw someone you liked and respected going through a dark time, but she knew Slay was right.

"Besides, less time working here means more time at home

with me," Slay said, bringing the conversation back around. "And Charlie."

Home with Slay and Charlie! Nothing better. And yet…

"And where will this home *be*, Daddy?" she teased.

Alice had agreed to move in with Slay just before Christmas, and for a person used to second-guessing herself, she was shocked at how easy that decision had been. Then again, maybe it wasn't *so* shocking, considering he'd asked her right after Pevrell and Brahms' winter concert, where Slay, dressed to the nines in a tailored suit and silk tie, had clapped louder and longer for Charlie than any of the other parents had for their children. But Alice *had* been surprised at how well-received her decision had been by everyone around them. It seemed like everyone realized just how right she and Slay were together.

Now the only fly in the ointment was the question of *where* they'd live. They'd discussed a variety of scenarios, but none of their options seemed quite right. Slay's place didn't have enough room for Charlie, and Alice's current house, while perfect in every other respect, was a rental, and Slay wanted to own.

Slay had told her to leave their housing situation up to him, and at first she'd almost laughed out loud. Let him pick a house? Alone? But he hadn't been joking. And Alice could now say with confidence that submitting to a blindfold was a hundred times easier than letting the man you love buy a home for you.

"Funny you should ask," he told her. "I signed an agreement and made a down payment today."

Alice pulled back to gape at him. "On New Year's Eve Day? You already signed a contract? Where is the place? When can I see it?"

Slay chuckled. "You've already seen it," he told her. "I called your landlord and asked if he was interested in selling. Turns out, property management is not his idea of a fun retirement, and he was happy to sell. Gave me a great price. And we can stay where we are."

"No way!" she breathed. "We get to stay?"

"Yup. Only adjustment we'll have to make is putting a lock on the back half of the basement and telling Charlie he can't go near my, uh, *exercise equipment*."

Alice laughed out loud. "That's perfect!" She threw her arms around his neck and he lifted her up to spin her around. His brown eyes smiled up at her, and she leaned down to rain kisses over his cheeks.

"Happy, baby?" he asked.

"*So* happy, Daddy," she told him.

"Wanna go tell the masses?"

She nodded. He set her on her feet and guided her inside with his hand on her lower back.

She opened the door to chaos, utter and complete chaos.

Donnie, a six-two, muscle-bound bouncer who'd worked at The Club for years, gave her a smile and Slay a chin lift as they walked in.

"This place is *packed*," Alice marveled.

For this one night only, the front bar was the most happening spot in The Club. Normally, this space was a completely generic, nondescript meeting place, a facade that hid the guarded doorway that led to The Club's main areas. But for New Year's Eve, thanks to the man at her side, this outer bar had been transformed… into a 1970s disco, complete with mirror ball, DJ, and dance floor.

And in the middle of that dance floor, encased in a purple, sparkly dress and doing her best Dancing Queen impression, was none other than Slay's neighbor, Betty.

Alice turned and buried her head in Slay's chest. "You're really the best, you know that, Daddy?" she said, fighting back a laugh.

Before Slay could answer, Betty had caught sight of them.

"Alexander Slater, you owe me a drink!" she called from the middle of the floor.

"Jesus," Slay muttered under his breath. "I've already bought her *three*."

Alice collapsed into giggles.

"And you there!" Betty called again, beckoning towards them. "You! With all the muscles!"

Slay and Alice looked at one another, and then swiveled their heads together in shock to look at Donnie, who had turned rather pale.

"Come back and *dance* again!" Betty yelled with a shake of her hips.

Donnie shook his head and waved a hand in denial. "Nope, I'm all set, ma'am. Thanks anyway."

"Come on!" Betty yelled again.

"Better go, man," Slay told Donnie with a straight face.

Donnie's expression darkened as he looked at Slay. "Slay, man, I've already been out there, and she—"

"Donnie, she's a sweet old lady," Matteo said, walking over to clap Slay on the shoulder, a mischievous smile on his face. "Christ. Be a gentleman."

"But—"

"Afraid this old lady has more *moves* than you do?" Betty taunted.

Donnie took a deep breath and glared at Slay. "You owe me," he said. Then he turned to Matteo, "And if she pinches my ass again, both of you are on my shit list." And then he stalked out to the dance floor.

"Finally!" Betty cried as Donnie approached, then she reached over and delivered a firm smack to Donnie's ass.

Alice slapped a hand over her mouth. "Holy crap! He's gonna hate both of you forever!"

Matteo and Slay looked at one another. "Worth it," they laughed in unison.

"You boys don't wanna lose me a bouncer," warned a deep

voice from behind them. "Not when I'm already about to lose one of my favorite waitresses."

Master Blake and Matteo's brothers Dom and Tony joined them, and Blake stepped over to greet Alice with a kiss on the cheek. "How are you honey?" he asked.

"I'm better than I've ever been," she replied, and he smiled, though the smile didn't quite reach his eyes.

"Quite an event you organized, Slay," Blake continued, looking around the bar. Easily a hundred people crowded the small space and the line at the bar was extensive. "The rest of The Club is dead. Everyone wants to be out here watching your friend Betty corrupt the bouncers."

Slay chuckled. "I knew I couldn't take her into The Club itself or else everyone at her hair salon would be getting the blow by blow on how to use a flogger."

"The *blow by blow*?" Tony asked, deadpan.

Slay rolled his eyes and Matteo groaned in disgust.

"Oh, come on! I didn't *make* the pun, I just *called him* on it!" Tony said, holding up his hands in protest.

"I think Mom dropped you on your head too many times," Dom told him, shaking his head and making Alice giggle.

"Where are Tess and the other girls?" Alice asked.

Tony scowled. "Ladies room out here was too crowded, so they headed back in there," he said, hooking a thumb towards the door that led to the main club. "Like, over twenty minutes ago. I'm not too worried since she's with the rest of the girls: Heidi, Hillary, and Slay's sister. But still, think you could go back there and hurry them up?"

Slay blinked and immediately stood straighter. "You mean *Elena*? My sister *Elena* is back there?"

"You have a different sister I don't know about?" Tony asked. "Yes, *Elena* is back there."

It was Slay's turn to scowl. "*Shit*. I brought her because I was concerned about Betty, and Elena's a nurse. I thought if Betty needed medical attention or anything…"

From the dance floor, they heard Betty cry, "Shake what your mama gave you, big boy!" and Tony and Matteo both burst into loud guffaws.

"Good thing you took that precaution," Matt said, wiping tears from his eyes. "Betty sure won't need her help, but Donnie might."

"Jesus," Slay muttered lifting a hand to rub the back of his neck. "I didn't want Elena to see the main area any more than I wanted Betty back there!"

Blake put a restraining hand on Slay's shoulder when Slay would have moved toward the main club. "Your sister doesn't look like the sort to run a tutorial at the beauty parlor," Blake said dryly. "Not quite the right demographic. Leave her be."

Slay scowled. "But Blake, she's way too young…"

"Wait, she told me she's twenty-six," Alice said, confused. "How old is she?"

"Twenty-six," Slay agreed irritably.

Allie pressed her lips together to bite back a smile. "And you know I'm *twenty-three*, right?"

Slay opened his mouth and closed it again. "Of course I know. That's different, Allie," he grumbled.

"I see," she said, patting his chest soothingly. Watching her man turn into a protective Neanderthal around his sister turned Alice's insides to mush. "Well, if you want, I'll go hurry her along. Escort her out with my hands over her eyes, maybe?"

Slay raised one eyebrow and gave her a look that said he'd noticed her sass, and Alice's tummy flipped even as she giggled.

But as it turned out, she didn't have to hurry the girls along, since they pushed their way through the crowd at that very moment.

Dom's eyes found Heidi immediately, and he reached out a

hand to draw his wife to his side. "All good?" he asked, leaning down to press a kiss to her forehead.

"Totally," Heidi agreed happily, exchanging a look with Tess.

Tess bit her lip around her smile and leaned into Tony's arm, letting him tangle his fingers through her long auburn hair. "Everything's *great,*" Tess sighed.

Alice frowned and looked at Hillary, who had buried her face in Matteo's chest while his arms wrapped protectively around her, so that only the top of her red-brown hair was visible.

Something was going on and it was on the tip of Alice's tongue to ask *what*… when Elena spoke.

"So, question. How does the whole rope bondage thing work?" she asked, pushing a strand of her long black hair behind her ear and looking expectantly from couple to couple. "*Shibari,* I think it's called? It looks super interesting."

Nobody spoke for several seconds. Blake cleared his throat once as though he might speak, then fell silent. Tony, Dom, and Matt made a careful study of the ceiling, the wall, and the floor, respectively. The girls exchanged speculative looks.

"How. The. *Hell.* do you know what shibari is?" Slay exploded.

Elena rolled her dark brown eyes, looking so exactly like Slay that Alice had to fight a bubble of completely inappropriate laughter that threatened to escape.

"Alex, I'm a twenty-six-year-old woman with an internet connection. I know a *lot* of things," she said matter-of-factly. "But I've only ever seen pictures, I've never seen it in real life, and I was curious about how it *felt*, you know?"

Slay looked like his head was about to explode. Alice stood on her tiptoes and wrapped her arms around his neck cautiously. "Slay, it's okay to be curious," she whispered.

He glanced at her briefly, nodded, and proceeded to ignore her.

"It had better just be idle curiosity, Elena," Slay warned, his jaw locked as he glared at his sister.

"It's none of your business if it's *idle* curiosity or *active* curiosity, Alex!" Elena said hotly. "You're my brother, *not* my keeper. I don't ask you about your sex life, and you don't get to ask about mine!"

"Guys," Tony said, putting out a placating hand towards Slay. "Cool it."

"Wh— But— That's because you're not supposed to *have* a sex life!" Slay sputtered.

"Slay, man, chill," Matteo said, his voice deep and threaded with humor.

"Oh, for heaven's sake," Elena fumed. "That's the stupidest thing you've ever said, and you've said some pretty stupid—"

"Stupid! It's not stupid to want to protect your baby sister!"

"Slay," Alice said, grabbing Slay around the waist. "Honey, calm…"

"But I don't *need* protection, Alex! I'm not—"

"I'M PREGNANT!"

Those words, screamed at the exact moment that the DJ turned the music down to announce that it was five minutes until midnight, did what no one else had been able to do. Slay and Elena both stopped yelling and swiveled their heads. In fact, everyone in the entire room turned to locate the source of this pronouncement.

Hillary, face flaming, gave a small wave, cleared her throat, and elaborated. "Elena said it sounds like I'm around ten weeks."

Tess, Heidi, and Elena looked thrilled, and not at all surprised. Hillary herself seemed overjoyed. Tony, Dom, and Slay, on the other hand, looked stunned. And Matteo, the man who always had a plan and was never caught on the back foot? He was completely poleaxed.

Hillary peeped up at him and grinned. "I *told* you I might be."

"Y-you said it was a *slim possibility*. You know I never spend time worrying about shit that *might* happen," he croaked, pulling her closer. "But it… it's definite?"

Hillary nodded. "Elena volunteers at the Women's Health Clinic. She has all kinds of STD tests and condoms and stuff in her car, and some pregnancy tests, too. I told her all my symptoms and she had me take one in the bathroom just now."

"It's absolutely positive," Elena confirmed, smiling. "I just told Hillie that she should follow up with her OB/GYN after the holiday, get an appointment for some routine tests, start taking a prenatal vitamin…"

"Fuck me," Matteo said wonderingly. Then he pointed a finger and glared at Slay and Elena in turn. "You two, stop your shit. My girl is pregnant and she can't be upset!" Then he frowned down at Hillary. "We need to get you home! We should never have come out. Christ, there are so many *people*," he said, frowning around at the crowd of innocent revelers.

"Matt, I'm *fine*," Hillie protested. "Just a little tired."

Elena nodded. "That's totally normal at this stage of the—"

"Tinker Bell, why the hell didn't you say so?" Matteo demanded. He bent down and scooped Hillary up into his arms.

"Matteo Angelico, you put me down!" Hillary demanded, though her demands fell on deaf ears, of course.

"From what I've seen," Elena told Hillie with a wink, "the alpha-caveman father-to-be is also a normal part of the process. Just enjoy it, sweetie."

"Everyone, out of the way!" Matteo yelled to the crowd, carrying Hillary towards the back.

"Congratulations, Hillie!" Alice yelled. "Call me!"

Hillary rolled her eyes and smiled over Matt's shoulder. "I will, I promise. Looks like I might be shackled to my bed until July, but he'll *probably* let me use the phone," she joked. She blew a kiss to her sister and waved goodbye to the others.

"Well, Hillary can't drink, but I say we have a toast in her honor," Blake said, stepping forward to lead everyone to the bar. "On the house!" Tess linked her arm through Elena's, making sure that she was included in the group.

Slay noticed and frowned.

"Slay," Alice said, putting a hand on his hard chest to hold him back. "Let her have fun. No one's going to steal Elena's virtue in the middle of a crowded club. Though Blake *might* answer her shibari questions," she teased.

Slay drew Alice more tightly into his arms. "I notice you're getting pretty sassy with Daddy, Allie-girl," he said, his voice deep and rough.

"Maybe a little?" she admitted, feeling the familiar tug in her belly that always came when he spoke in that voice.

He nodded slowly, his hot eyes roaming her face. "I could take you upstairs, find a free room, take care of that problem for you."

"Your sister might wonder where we are," Alice reminded him, her heart beating faster, half hoping he'd do it anyway.

Slay's eyes came to rest on hers. "You think I'm being over-protective of her?"

Alice pursed her lips and pretended to think about it. "Hmmm… just this much?" she said, holding her thumb and forefinger up an inch apart.

Slay sighed. "She's my little sister," he said simply. "My responsibility."

"I know," Alice agreed. "But it's okay for her to want some-thing *more*, you know? Something for herself. Something like what we have?"

Slay threw another dark look at his sister, and then focused on Alice. His eyes softened. "Yeah," he agreed. And then his eyes heated. "As soon as midnight comes, we're leaving," he pronounced. "We're going back to our own home to ring in the new year *my way*."

Alice felt a delicious chill slide up her spine and she pressed herself more firmly against his chest, knowing for certain that his arms would tighten around her, and loving when they did.

"You with me, baby?" Slay demanded.

"Always, Daddy," Alice whispered. "Always."

The End

Jane Henry

USA Today bestselling author Jane Henry pens stern but loving alpha heroes, feisty heroines, and emotion-driven happily-ever-afters. She writes what she loves to read: kink with a tender touch. Jane is a hopeless romantic who lives on the East Coast with a houseful of children and her very own Prince Charming.

Don't miss these exciting titles by Jane Henry and Blushing Books!

A Thousand Yesses

Bound to You series
Begin Again, Book 1
Come Back To Me, Book 2
Complete Me, Book 3

Boston Doms Series
By Jane Henry and Maisy Archer
My Dom, Book 1
His Submissive, Book 2
Her Protector, Book 3
His Babygirl, Book 4
His Lady, Book 5
Her Hero, Book 6
My Redemption, Book 7

Anthologies

Hero Undercover
Sunstrokes

Connect with Jane Henry
janehenrywriter.blogspot.com
janehenrywriter@gmail.com

Maisy Archer

Maisy is an unabashed book nerd who has been in love with romance since reading her first Julie Garwood novel at the tender age of 12. After a decade as a technical writer, she finally made the leap into writing fiction several years ago and has never looked back. Like her other great loves - coffee, caramel, beach vacations, yoga pants, and her amazing family - her love of words has only continued to grow... in a manner inversely proportional to her love of exercise, house cleaning, and large social gatherings. She loves to hear from fellow romance lovers, and is always on the hunt for her next great read.

Don't miss these exciting titles by Jane Henry and Maisy Archer with Blushing Books!

Boston Doms Series
By Jane Henry and Maisy Archer
My Dom, Book 1
His Submissive, Book 2
Her Protector, Book 3
His Babygirl, Book 4
His Lady, Book 5
Her Hero, Book 6
My Redemption, Book 7

Anthologies
Hero Undercover
Sunstrokes

Connect with Maisy Archer
janeandmaisy.com

Blushing Books

Blushing Books is one of the oldest eBook publishers on the web. We've been running websites that publish spanking and BDSM related romance and erotica since 1999, and we have been selling eBooks since 2003. We hope you'll check out our hundreds of offerings at http://www.blushingbooks.com.

Lightning Source UK Ltd.
Milton Keynes UK
UKHW010742060223
416537UK00003B/941